£ 1
8/23

i

c

o

p

e

EVERYONE GETS EATEN

BEN BROOKS

Billions:
    Full town meeting.
    Mandatory.
    Salmon pink.
    Be calm.

President Captain blinked. He looked out at the citizens of Billion, assembled before him on rows of blue plastic chairs. They were all between the ages of four and six. President Captain was five and a half. He was the fourth oldest, second lightest, and fifth most talented thrower of clocks.

He coughed and the microphone between his hands squealed feedback. President Captain was more afraid than anyone of the oncoming night. It made him strong. He rarely slept for anything longer than three minutes. When he did manage to drift off, he dreamed of tigers and inadvertently began to pound his wife between the eyes.

Lucille Captain was sitting on the back row, her chair atop a dream encyclopedia in order to make herself clearly visible. Focusing solely on his wife was the only way President Captain managed to complete an address without regular breaks in which he climbed beneath the stage and curled up, making lost whale sounds and chewing his toenails. He stared at the purple islands on her forehead and took a deep breath.

'Good morning,' he said, not loud enough to dispel the cloud of chat that filled the hall. He made a dial-twisting motion at the sound engineer. 'Good morning,' he said again. This time his voice was vast. People settled into quiet, ran back to their own chairs, and removed fingers from each other's nostrils.

'As you maybe know already, a thing happened early today and it happened by the planetarium and it's definitely nothing to be scared about so don't cry. Keep breathing, thumbs in mouths, picture a beach in the Maldives.' He paused and took his own advice. 'Okay, listen, Tatiana P was going home this morning when—'

He paused. Lucille nodded to him. He wanted to press his fists against his ears in anticipation of the sounds that would follow. 'She was attacked by a T-Rexasaurus.'

The hall erupted.

Shoes were thrown.

Bare feet stomped the floorboards.

Six people fainted.

The butcher vomited.

Tatiana P wept.

As the mayor winced and the people screamed, Casper Font sat cross-legged at stage left, turning a plastic owl over in his hands. He was trembling. The plan no longer seemed watertight. It had barely begun and already he felt it filling with holes. He felt guilty. It was obvious that people would take the sudden re-emergence of dinosaurs as an omen. They would think that the night was approaching. He didn't know anything about that. He guessed that it might be.

'Burn the T-Rexasaurus!' someone shouted.

'Burn the mayor!' someone else shouted.

'Take the mayor's shoes!'

'Leave the mayor alone.'

'Yes,' Captain President said. 'Leave the mayor alone. I'm trying my best and that's all that counts. I've located the last living Dinosaur Hunter. He's here now. Casper, could you come up?'

Casper got unsteadily to his feet and shuffled onto the stage. Captain President passed him the microphone, took two steps back, and drew a finger across his throat. The people fell silent.

'Okay,' Casper said, balling his hands in his pockets. 'It's all probably maybe going to be okay.'

He scanned the audience until he found Tatiana P. Bright, shiny, Tatiana. Tatiana, who, when they'd first met, had slid her finger into his nose as they sat by the canal folding origami fortunetellers from sugar paper. Tatiana who, when she found out how everyone else saw him, immediately lost interest and began putting her fingers into the noses of boys with bigger houses, hearts, and forearms.

No one alive then could remember a time when there had been dinosaurs in Billion. This meant Casper had forever sat with empty hands. There was no place for him. He slept in a hill of cardboard beyond The Clay Modeling District. In cold times, he covered himself with scraps of clay discarded by the sculptors and slept with his hands pinned in his armpits.

Casper hadn't said anything for fifteen seconds.

The crowd were restless.

A flying shoe struck his temple.

'Have you ever even killed a dinosaur?' someone shouted.

Casper reddened. 'No, Kevin, you know I never killed a dinosaur. When have you ever seen me kill a dinosaur?'

'Then how are you a dinosaur hunter?'

'My family are dinosaur hunters. It's what we do. Your family make milk.'

'Don't take that tone, hollowhead. You're at the bar more than anyone.'

The mayor arched his eyebrows. Casper mouthed *sorry*. He rolled his head and shook his hands as though preparing for a sprint. 'Even though I've never killed a dinosaur, I've been taught about it since I was even smaller than this. I can do it. I will do it. It's what I was always supposed to do. I will punch down the T-Rexasaurus and keep the stupid night away.'

Casper was surprised at his own volume. The mayor clapped and the people followed.

'Burn the Rexasaurus!' Sally Wills shouted.

'Don't burn the mayor!' Someone shouted.

Neil Vess stood, raised his hand and split his fingers into live long and prosper. 'May the force be with you,' he shouted.
'Sit down, Neil,' Ryan Vess said, pulling his brother by the belt loops.

'Where did the penguins go?' Angelica Nguyen asked, climbing first over, then under her chair.

'Quiet,' Captain President said, taking back the microphone.

'Quiet,' Captain President said again, making a steering wheel motion at the sound engineer.

They listened.

His voice hurt their ears.

'I've promised you that nothing bad will happen. We will crush the T-Rexasaurus, and any dinosaurs that are friends with it. We are Billions and we will hit the night in its soft parts until it cries and leaves forever.' He exhaled and thumbed the gap between his eyebrows. 'There are revised copies of *The Dinosaur Manual* under each of your seats. Continue as normal.'

A,

I'm in a hospital. In Spain. I'm not sure why. I've been told I have a destructive personality. I can't sit still. Last year, I surrendered my shoes to two muggers without being asked. They might not have been muggers. They said they wanted telephone change.

Pedro said I was jumping between balconies. And that I smashed a window to climb inside an apartment that wasn't my apartment. I don't remember that. I don't remember much. They've given me diazepam. I'm still not asleep. They gave me more. I'm just not sleepy.

This email is coming from nowhere. I know that. I'm sorry. I checked and the last time we emailed was five years ago. It was a chain email. It said that if you didn't forward the email to fifteen people then a ghost horse would come into your bedroom and steal all your tomorrows. I forwarded the email to thirty people. I just wanted to be safe.

I don't think you're going to reply to this. It's okay. But I wanted to tell someone where I was.

When I try to imagine where you are I always imagine one of those houses with glass walls. Somewhere cold. By water. Lake Como? And you're cracking your knuckles. And a broad-shouldered man is telling you not to crack your knuckles. And you're telling the broad-shouldered man you can crack whatever you want to crack. Then you smash a teapot.

A nurse just came in. She couldn't speak English. I can't speak Spanish. She made me take off my shirt and she attached plastic nodes to various parts of my body. When I took off my shirt she read the tattoo on my belly out loud and very slowly. It says *fuck everything*. It's very possible I shouldn't have a tattoo that says that. Still, it's there. The nurse had beautiful eyes and she smelled like lasagna. She's gone now.

I got the tattoo done with a girl who is the Spanish voice of

Natalie Portman. Every time Natalie Portman's voice is over-dubbed into Spanish, it's Leti. Leti is impulsive. Not in the road trip sort of way. At 3am one night we were drinking Negrita and she said we should get tattoos from her friend with sewing needles so we did.

It hurt to have sex afterwards. I told Leti I wish that I'd be crushed to death by wildebeest. I've been thinking a lot about that. Because of Lion King. I had a dream you were crushed to death by wildebeest too. Can you confirm this? How did it feel? I tried to save you. Honestly. It was out of my hands.

Recently I've been trying to wake up while I'm asleep. It's hard. In my book about dreams it says you can work out if you're dreaming or not by pressing a light switch. If the light switch turns the light on you are not dreaming. There are never any light switches in my dreams.

It's eighty-five degrees outside. The woman next to me is about to die. I think she'll be dead by tomorrow. She looks so bored. She keeps making donkey sounds. Honestly. She's braying.

I think I'm going to be asleep soon,

C

One.

Do not approach dinosaurs.

Do not shout disparaging remarks at dinosaurs.

Do not, even in the privacy of your own homes, make jokes about dinosaurs.

Do not, even in your dreams, attempt to wrestle dinosaurs.

Do not attempt to placate dinosaurs with offerings of milk or unwanted siblings.

Do not draw dinosaurs.

Do not curl up and cry late at night, after three cartons of milk, imagining dinosaurs pulling you apart like wet paper.

Do not pull each other apart like wet paper over arguments concerning the nature of dinosaurs.

Do not concern yourself with the nature of dinosaurs.

Do not ask the people above the clouds for help with dinosaurs.

Do not blink in the presence of dinosaurs.

Just don't.

Okay?

*

In The Doll Hospital, Casper watched Dr Sixteen press his stethoscope against the chest of a plastic baby. The doctor closed his eyes and shook his head. Casper sipped milk. He was sitting on an empty bed, swinging his heels into the metal frame.

'Stop it,' Sixteen said.

'Sorry,' Casper said, not stopping. 'Are you going to tell me what to do?'

'No. I'm not going to tell you what to do. You should have asked what to do before you did what you did.'

Casper squinted as though it would help him understand. Sixteen was only four and a quarter but he spoke like someone double that. They had been close for three years. Casper was often falling into holes and Sixteen was often pulling him out of them. Sometimes, never purposely, Casper would push his friend into holes and find himself totally unable to help him climb out. That always made his stomach sink.

The doctor moved along to the next bed, again pressing his stethoscope to pretend pink skin and listening intently. Casper raised his voice. 'They want to give me a new house.'

'I'm trying to work.'

'In The Meatball District.'

'Are you going to take it?'

'No.'

'Good.'

'Why good?'

'Because when this ends how it will inevitably end, they'll be less upset if you haven't accepted whatever dumb gifts they're offering.'

Casper tipped a long stream of milk down his throat, placed the carton on the bedside table, and lay down. 'It might not end like that.'

'If it doesn't end like that, we can swap houses.'

'You'll live in The Cardboard Hill?'

'If I'm wrong.'

Casper opened his mouth to reply, stopping himself as a junior nurse sidled up to Sixteen and presented him with a clipboard. On the clipboard was a red heart drawn above a flat black line. She pointed at a cot in one corner of the room. The doctor nodded and passed back the clipboard.

'What did it say?'

'Same as it always says.'

A door swung shut as the junior nurse disappeared. Casper rolled onto his front. 'Have you told Diana?'

Diana was Sixteen's wife. She worked as a fireman in The Origami Quarter and still believed in the voices above the clouds. She disliked her husband's only friend and encouraged their disentanglement. It wasn't that Casper seemed particularly bad, just that he never expressed concern or care for anything. She wanted him to care about something, anything, even if it was only fish spotting or sketching charcoal doodles of his own feet.

'Absolutely not. If she knew, I wouldn't get to play with you at all.'

'You never play with me at all anyway.' He drained the last of his milk. 'Come down to the bar.'

'I can't. I have a job.'

'I'm trying to get a job. I'm making a job for myself.'

'You're not trying to get a job. You're trying to get a girl.'

Casper stared at the ceiling, picturing Tatiana and then George. His future with Tatiana was resting on the shoulders of George. Tiny, shaky George, who didn't know left from right and could only count up to fourteen. The only person he knew who would agree to the plan. The only person capable of spectacularly ruining the plan.

'Can I ask something?' The doctor said, hanging the stethoscope from his neck and turning to face his one friend.

'Yes.'

'Why did you suddenly decided to do this? You never said about doing this before. It's been a long time since Tatiana didn't want to sit next to you.'

One of Casper's shoes nudged the either. His gaze locked onto them. 'She's connected to Kevin now. I watched by the cathedral, they were in each other's noses.'

*

The sky slid from pink to orange as one set of presenters left the radio tower and a new set arrived. Avery and Pele liked to count the steps out loud and in unison as they ascended them. There were one hundred and eighty-four. Another thing they liked to do was knock each other down.

Pele jabbed his elbow into the back of Avery's knee. Avery collapsed. He stood up. He was wearing shorts. A drawbridge of skin hung open from his knee.

'What did you do that for?'

'What do you mean? We always kick each other.'

Pele had been eating a bacon double cheeseburger. Avery had been pulling splinters from the sides of his fingernails with his teeth.

'We don't kick each other anymore. There are dinosaurs now. It's not appropriate.'

Pele took a bite the size of a lemon, releasing a trickle of brown grease down his chin. He replied with a full mouth. 'There aren't dinosaurs.'

Avery took a step back. 'Yes there are. And the night is coming.'

'People always say 'the night is coming.' What does that even mean? It's stupid. I don't see any night.'

'That's the point, you don't see it until it's here. Everything turns so slowly grey that you don't notice it until it's not grey anymore.'

'That won't happen.'

'Yes, it will.'

With a karate chop, Avery knocked the burger from his co-host's hands.

'That was my burger.'

'Don't brag.'

'What?'

'We're late.'

In silence, they continued climbing until they reached The Globe. The Globe was a giant glass ball containing the radio studio and a members-only café patronized by business owners and councilmen. At two hundred feet, it was the tallest building in Billion, as well as the most expensive and most frequently insulted (the bald ghost, the blob, the worst stupidest thing ever made by anyone ever, and so on).

The producer nodded to them as they fell into mono-grammed swivel chairs and donned oversized headphones. Neither presenter returned the nod. Skull-sized mugs of Darjeeling appeared before them. They waited for the crossover track to play out then began to talk.

'You're listening to Nine FM with Pele Marti—'

'And Avery Vitafit. The sky is currently mint green, there are fourteen clouds, and it's shorts weather.'

'No, it isn't.'

'Yes, it is.'

'You're wearing shorts and you have goosebumps.'

'Because you pushed me onto marble steps, you table.'

'That isn't how you get goosebumps.'

'It is, if you have sensitive—'

The producer took them off air, replacing their voices with a short pre-recorded documentary about active volcanoes in Japan. He asked what was going on. Before they answered, he told them that he didn't care what was going on. He told them to shove whatever was going on up themselves and pull it back out of their ear holes. He asked if they wanted to keep their boxy villas and their pedal cars. They told him they did. They agreed to surrender. They averted each other's eyes and sipped tea.

The pair had been working on the radio show for a year. In that year, they had only fought twice. Once when Pele pushed Avery from the top of the tower after seeing what he thought was a mattress and believing that his friend would simply bounce back up. Another time when Avery took a hoax call seriously and informed the entire town of an imminent jellyfish hurricane.

Teal green. The first caller of the night came in. It was a six year old who slept beside the canal and tickled trout.

'First caller! What's your name and where are you from?'

'Shape. The canal.'

'Shape, The Canal, what would you like to say to the listeners?'

A pause and rustling. 'The night is coming,' he said. 'I am

seeing very many giant knees. I am hearing voices from above the clouds. They are talking of shampoo and peanuts. Hullaballoo. Shenanigans. They say that. They are saying such things.'

Pele pushed fingers into his mouth to cork a laugh. Avery glared at him. 'What else did the voices say?'

'They are talking always like clocks. They talk about the clocks. They talk about us. They call the clock tosses idiot dumb stuff. They make the squelching sounds. They make sounds like feet in tomato muck. Squelch.'

Pele let out his laughter and Avery jammed an elbow into that open mouth.

*

Casper entered the milk bar to applause and unopened milk cartons shoved between his hands. He remembered what Sixteen had said and ordered his own. He sat on an upturned bucket at the bar, staring through the glass ceiling at the orange sky. Slim fingers of cloud divided it into wide bands. He thought of Diana yelling at him across a dinner table about the voices in the sky. He thought of himself slouching and falling asleep in a bath of ball-size bubbles.

A loud gang kettled him.

'How will you kill it?'

'What will you use?'

'Can you really do it?'

'Should we be hiding?'

'Not now,' he said. 'I'm tired.'

The Vess twins attempted to empty the area around him. 'The Dinosaur Hunter needs personal space,' they chanted. When a space was cleared, the three of them sat and played Yahtzee until Casper got tired of all the eyes, and excused himself, swaying out into the deep orange.

He didn't want to go back to The Cardboard Hill. He didn't

want to be alone. He wanted to sit somewhere and panic and drink milk uninterrupted.

The milk bar, the main milk bar, was in The Circle, next to city hall and the mayor's office and the cathedral. There were other bars, in the fringes of Billion. Casper rarely visited them. They made him feel unsafe. They were full of people like him. People who didn't slot in anywhere and had to cling to edges of whatever giant rotating world they were supposed to be existing on.

He walked for an hour through The Confetti District and Little Uganda and Elmbridge, to The Queen's, a bar he'd once hidden in while trying to escape revelers at The Tentacle Festival.

The Queen's was empty except for its barman and Ned Kloot. During his previous visit, the barman had told Casper everything he knew about Ned Kloot. Casper didn't know why. Casper hadn't asked.

Ned had played the pachinko machine beside the woman's toilet door for twelve hours every day for three years. None of the balls he won were ever been exchanged for anything. They were kept in the basement of his house on The Street of Not Sleeping. He was collecting an inheritance for a son that he didn't have. He had a feeling he sometimes described as being 'in his knees' that he definitely did have a son, somewhere, and that one day the son would return, wearing mohair and softly crying.

'You don't look like you looked earlier,' the barman said. 'You look smaller.' He didn't say it in an unfriendly way. He said it like a pat on the arm.

'Um,' Casper said. 'I don't know. The whole town is looking at me.'

'What do you expect? You're the dinosaur hunter and now there are dinosaurs. You've got something to do. A place. You should be glad.'

'I'm not a dinosaur hunter. I never killed a dinosaur.'

The barman clicked off the radio. It had been irritating that night, consisting mostly of the presenters maliciously nicknaming each other after sea mammals. 'You haven't killed a dinosaur *yet*.'

'What if something goes wrong?'

He winked. 'Then everyone will be eaten there will be no one left to blame you.' He turned and filled a pint glass with strawberry milkshake, then set it before Casper and told him to keep his hands out of his pockets. He leaned in. 'If you're worried, you should go see The Dream Nurse. She'll tell you what to expect.'

Casper stared into his glass. He looked up and over the barman's shoulder at a chalkboard filled with cramped handwriting.

Chocolate for dreams of yesterday.

Banana for dreams of today.

Strawberry for dreams of tomorrow.

The barman was right. He needed to go and see The Dream Nurse. She'd be able to tell him whether or not to abort the plan. She could help. She wouldn't help. He couldn't go to The Dream Nurse. It was too complicated. Things between them had never healed. They were standing with their backs to each other on opposite sides of a deep fissure.

But what else?

He drained the glass in one, thanked the barman, nodded at Ned Kloot, and headed toward The Cardboard Hill.

*

'You can't kill a dinosaur. You don't know how.' Kevin scrunched his mouth in anger until his lips became white. Fizika winced. 'Okay, fine, you can kill a dinosaur.'

'I could kill a hundred dinosaurs if I had to.'

'You could kill a million!'

'Don't take that tone with me you idiot goose.'

Fizika raised his palms. 'I'm not taking any tone with anyone.'

'I'm sick of your obnoxious attitude.' Kevin flagged down a waiter in a tabard and ordered another round of sweet teas and a platter of fudge blocks. The waiter dipped his head in a shallow bow and disappeared.

Fizika silently mouthed 'obnoxious attitude?' as though to a camera crew hidden behind the bar.

They were sitting in The Kissing Hall at the edge of Elmbridge. Neither of them had done any kissing. Every time a girl approached, finger outstretched in search of a vacant nostril, Fizika straightened himself expectantly and Kevin made exaggerated shooing motions.

'How are you going to kill it?'

'I'll hit it, obviously.'

'Will that work?'

'I'll hit it hard. And with a bat. I bought a bat.'

'A bat?'

'Yes. Listen, what's wrong with you?'

'But it's going to be a dinosaur.'

Kevin uppercut Fizika in the armpit. 'I know it's going to be a dinosaur. What else is it going to be?'

'I know you know it's going to be a dinosaur.'

'Be quiet.'

Fizika claimed to need the toilet and excused himself. Kevin put his hands beneath his t-shirt and ran his palms over the ridges and bumps and splits. He felt the purple domes of Tatiana-shaped bruises. He pictured himself wearing a T-Rexasaurus head like a glove.

When Fizika returned, there were dribbles of green under each of his nostrils. Kevin snorted but said nothing. His companion had become relaxed and sleepy, slouching almost to the point of sliding from his seat.

'Why do you want to kill it so much? Won't it be dangerous? You should just leave it to that Casper teapot. Relax. Danger for strangers.'

'That isn't what that means.'

'Maybe not.'

'You don't understand anyway.'

'I do. He kissed Tatiana one time. It was an age ago. She won't go back to him just because he kills some dinosaur that probably isn't anywhere anyway.'

'He'll be the richest person in Billion.'

'And she'll leave?' Kevin shrugged and pulled his t-shirt up over his face like a mask. 'Even if you don't like it, he's the dinosaur hunter. It's his job. How would you get there before him?'

Kevin let his t-shirt drop. 'I have a plan.' He dropped a handful of numbers onto the table and left the kissing hall.

*

At home, Casper pulled *A Field Guide to Hunting Dinosaurs* from his pillowcase. He turned to the relevant page and read. He read it again. He pushed his nose against the lines of the drawing. He didn't know why. It wasn't necessary, but he felt like he wanted to pretend to kill it in the right way. The way his father had done. Even though no one would know any different.

*

George Stanza came from a long line of large handed men. His father had been a policeman with fists the size of bowling balls. His father's father had been a policeman with fists the size of boulders. When George was born, with eight fingers and a propensity for accruing bruises from inanimate objects, they bundled him in newspaper and left him on the other side of the town, in an abandoned shipping container that smelled of salt and salmon.

Four and a half years later, under the light of a single candle, George sat in the shipping container, opening and closing his miniature hands like mouths.

'Casper make you rich,' one hand said.

'Mayor make you jail,' the other replied.

'Rich means house.'

'Jail means boring.'

'House means people.'

'Jail means mean people.'

He sighed and stopped. He walked to one corner of the metal room and heaved aside a blue tarpaulin. Admittedly, it did look realistic. Or it at least looked like the pictures George had seen. Felt tip doodles on billboards and illuminated illustrations in old books.

The suit consisted of a giant bamboo frame with black latex stretched over it. Individual green scales covered it entirely. The eyes were giant marbles. The teeth were shards of glass.

George poked the sleeping dinosaur and made a low humming sound. He climbed into bed and didn't sleep.

*

It's useful to approach the slaying of dinosaurs as a form of puzzle solving. Each kill will require the hunter to complete a series of moves specific to each species. Even within individuals of a species there will be a degree of variance, meaning that the techniques set forth in this manual may need slight alteration.

The T-Rexasaurus is responsible for more known fatalities than all other species of dinosaur combined. Although not the largest of its kind, it houses between four and six hundred glass teeth as well as the ability to run faster than any train, making it a formidable opponent not to be underestimated.

The first stage of the slaying requires getting the beast horizontal, thus rendering it immobile and providing easy access to its head for the second stage. The second stage needs some kind of large, hard-edged object to be dropped into the jaw of the dinosaur. Lastly, the nostrils should be plugged, forcing the T-Rexasaurus to swallow the object, which will then become lodged in its throat, choking it to death.

Good luck.

A,

You didn't reply. I didn't think you'd reply. I'm sorry for carrying on. I'm bored of making myself bored. I'm selfish. I already knew that. Pedro told me again, after he got me out of the hospital. We were drinking beers and eating peanuts. He told me he was selfish too. Just quieter about it. And I should try to learn to do the same. I was holding a printout of my heartbeat.

I went back to the apartment I was staying in. The woman told me to leave. She was crying a lot. I wanted to touch her arm. And say nice things. I didn't. I think she would have hit me. I think she should have hit me. I hope she's okay.

I've lived with three people since I moved here. The first one got drunk and told me it was upsetting that I never left my room. It made her uneasy. The second one didn't get drunk. She just told me. She had sex a lot with a person who wore hemp clothes. I masturbated listening to their sounds through the wall. He was her brother. It turned out he sounds were coming from the elderly Russian couple next door. I didn't masturbate in that house again. I masturbated in the toilet of a bar that smelled like a junkyard.

Now I'm in a hotel room. At Hotel Tarraco. It's in the centre of Tarragona. Tarragona is on the east coast of Spain. By Barcelona. The reason I'm here is because I don't want to be anywhere else. Another reason is that I write. Books. Not very good ones. But ones. They exist now. Like marshmallows or the internet. And some of the people here like them. So there's that.

I wrote about us. Maybe you know that. People always ask how much is true. It makes me want to be asleep. I don't know how much is true. I don't know how I'd know that.

It's hard.

The sky right now is pink in a purple skirt.

I'm sitting in the window frame. Looking down. Drinking

a Peroni from the minibar. I bought oranges, rum, and Estrella too. I don't want to leave this room. Maybe ever. I'm trying to work out if this fall is high enough. I don't want to end up retarded. I think it's hard to buy drugs when you're retarded. And to hail taxis. I guess I could learn Murderball. And write a book about overcoming odds. I don't think I'm ever going to overcome any odds. Partly because I won't be faced with any. Partly because if I was, I'd go to bed,

C

Two.

After three hours of restless sleep, Casper rolled out of bed and poured himself a glass of milk. He drank it with a ball of stale liquorice, his forehead pressed to the tracing paper window. The sky beyond was beginning to give up its blue and don pink. Fuchsia. Morning.

He swallowed and shivered and thought of The Dream Nurse.

Casper and The Dream Nurse had been born in parallel cots. They had dammed streams together and hunted frogs together and hurled paper planes through clouds together. They learned to swim in the canal, dragged along by the eels gripped in their hands. They learned to climb on the edge of The Jungle, heaving each other up to low branches. They camped and cooked and wrestled. They caught moths and built castles. They were rarely separated by anything greater than an hour.

Then Casper met a girl at The Tentacle Festival. She saw how he skipped between rooftops and she assumed he'd have a title and she led him away.

After his encounter with Tatiana P, Casper no longer wanted to spend time with his childhood friend. He spent entire days in his cardboard hill, drawing faces on the walls and writing extensive accounts of that night by the canal. Initially, The Dream Nurse would come to him. She brought blackcurrants and cold toast. She made motivational speeches through the corrugated door. She told him who had won the clock tosses and who had lost the milk chugs. Eventually, she stopped coming. When Casper was dragged out of The Cardboard Hill by Dr Sixteen, the colour of clouds and the weight of a kitten, he knew that whatever had been between them was irreparable.

And now he would have to repair it if he wanted Tatiana back.

Back? He thought, as though repeating a question he hadn't fully heard.

The transistor radio hitched to Casper's grandfather clock switched itself on.

'You're listening to Nine FM with Keira Mary-Kate. The sky is currently fuchsia and the cloud count has yet to be completed, has it, Milo, you lazy sack of- A clock toss will be held today. Terra Cota. At the clock pitch. It's not mandatory, although there will be complimentary milk and an assortment of misshapen biscuits. The Dinosaur Hunter will be present.'

He really won't be, Casper thought.

'Reported dinosaur sightings have continued to flood in, from areas as far afield as Little New South Wales, Wirtschaft, and Kinkburton. Although none have yet been verified, they're all probably—'

Casper turned off the radio and pulled on a fleece. He carefully placed a sheet over his clock and left the cardboard hill.

Outside, the streets were empty. Squares of yellow had begun appearing in walls and plumes of smoke poked out of chimneys. The smell of baking bread made an entrance. A kettle whistled.

The station was a squat wooden building with three chipped wooden benches along each platform. He took a seat, blew hard onto his hands, and mentally rehearsed speeches.

I am the worst person in the world and I need your help. I am going to die if you don't help me. Do you want me to turn to dust in jail?

The train arrived and he boarded, the monologue in his head unrelenting. He kept his eyes on his feet.

I'm sorry for everything but if you don't translate my dream then you are murdering me. If you murder me, I will murder you back. Don't murder me, please. I'm asking you nicely.

Standing at her door, he wondered if there really was a possibility of him dying. Either immediately, as a result of complications arising from the plan, or later, in jail.

She answered the door in a frayed dressing gown, with a toothbrush in her hand and white foam at her lips. She looked vague. She didn't look like a person capable of catching frogs or building castles. Her new size rendered her unfamiliar.

'What?' she said. Her voice wasn't angry. Not because she wasn't angry, but because she didn't want to appear angry. She still thought about him, once every three days, and never quietly.

None of the prewritten speeches came out of his mouth. Instead, he held out a square of paper and whispered, 'please.'

'You want me to translate?'

'Yes.'

'Your dream?'

'Yes.'

'You think I'll say yes?'

He shifted his weight from one foot to the other, then back again. 'I don't know.'

She catapulted her toothbrush and hit him between the eyes. It stung like a hornet. She slammed the door. Casper balled up his dream and dropped it into the crabgrass. He left.

*

When she felt the bed rise slightly from the absence of Kevin's weight, Tatiana P retrieved the squirrel skull from beneath her pillow. She placed her thumbs in its eye sockets. She pressed her nose to the moon-coloured bone.

Tatiana hadn't killed the squirrel, only beheaded its corpse and boiled the head. It reminded her of things it was useful to be reminded of. It reminded her of her own skeleton and the fact that eventually it would be all that was left. It reminded her of other people's skeletons too, and that all she had to do was sporadically shove them in order to keep herself as herself for as long as possible.

Her mother had been mauled by a Rottweiler.

Her father had drowned in a koi pond.

Tatiana P was going to do neither of those things. She

jogged every morning, practiced plane-noise yoga, and had the coordination of an aerial acrobat.

Kevin was in the kitchen, arranging scrambled eggs and bacon and chunks of chocolate on a tray painted with cartoon dogs. He filled a mug half full of tea and topped it up with milk and added six sugars. He peeled an orange and tore apart the segments and arranged them in the shape of a crescent moon.

She hid the skull when he entered. He carefully set the food down on her lap. Her hand twitched as he held out the tea, sending a drop out to cling to her eyelash. She seized his forearm.

'Do you like that?' she said, forcing further splashes out of the cup and onto his chest.

'Please.' He didn't resist. 'Tatiana.'

'You don't like that. Do you? I don't like it either.' She hurled the mug at the ceiling where it smashed to dust and fell into their hair like powder snow.

I will fight monsters for you, Kevin thought.

'Make me more,' Tatiana screamed.

*

Deaf Paul had woken up lonely, with a streaming nose and clicking in his ears, and as a result was causing commotion at the meeting of the mayor's council. Deaf Paul was nearly one hundred percent deaf. He was also the tallest person in Billion and the only person never to have caught a pigeon with his bare hands.

'Objection!' Deaf Paul said, slapping Elgar.

'You don't even know what he said,' Simeon replied.

'Objection!' Deaf Paul said again, slapping Simeon.

Captain President slammed his fist into the table. 'Why does everyone think you have to slap the person when you object? That's not a rule. I told you all that wasn't a rule anymore.'

'Sorry.'

'Sorry.'

'Good.'

Deaf Paul raised his hand to object but Simeon caught him by the wrist and twisted. Deaf Paul didn't know they called him that. He guessed that if he had a nickname, it was likely Tall Paul, which was what he signed himself as on joining day.

'Why is he still on the council?'

'He's useful.'

'He's not useful. He's just big.'

'Obj—'

Deaf Paul fell silent as Casper entered the room. Captain President grinned and saluted. The others followed.

It was the first time Casper had seen the council chamber. The ceiling was vaulted stone, six times his height. The table was a slab of mahogany. The chairs were thrones with high backs and lopsided zebra faces carved into the armrests.

'Have a seat.'

'Um.'

Casper chose one of the head seats, farthest away from everyone else, directly opposite the mayor. He ran his hands along the underside of the table and found several blocks of hardened gum.

'Ready for the clock toss?' Captain President asked.

'I don't think I can go. I have other things to do. Dinosaur-related things.'

Captain President simultaneously shook his head and right forefinger. 'You have to go. It's good for morale. Morale is low.'

'I can't.'

'They like you. You're inspiring.'

Casper didn't feel inspiring. He felt false and blurry at the edges.

'I don't feel inspiring.'

'You will.'

'Um.'

'You should hear our plan. We have a plan. For when it returns.'

'I guess.'

The plan was that watchers would be stationed at each of the abandoned watchtowers in Billion. As soon as the T-Rex-asaurus was spotted, the watcher would sprint directly to The Dinosaur Hunter and inform him. The Dinosaur Hunter was to sleep in Hotel Ponzi so as to be easily reachable. The Dinosaur Hunter was to sleep only for fifteen minutes at a time. Casper tried to protest but was ignored.

The mayor opened his hands like a book. 'So,' he said. 'Let's talk numbers.'

'I don't want numbers.'

He didn't need numbers. One dead dinosaur would be enough. One dead dinosaur and one Tatiana P.

'You'll have numbers.'

'I'll give the numbers back.'

The council spoke behind raised hands amongst themselves. They picked at their noses and stamped the carpet. Elgar fixed a coin of gum to the table. A throat was cleared.

'We won't let you.'

'No deal.'

'You'll take the numbers.'

'Why don't you want numbers anyway?' Simeon's head hurt. He had more numbers than he could spend and he still wanted more numbers. He wanted all of the numbers. He didn't know why. He guessed he might take baths in them. 'You'll be able to move out of that cardboard cave.'

Casper balled his hands in his pockets and tensed his feet. He couldn't think of a reason. He could only think of Dr Sixteen, twirling his stethoscope like a baton. 'Okay,' he said. 'I'll take numbers.'

*

To be paid by the town of Billion to Casper Font following his successful slaying of the T-Rexasaurus that made Tatiana P cry and everyone very scared:

Ten thousand numbers.

Four parachutes (red).

Unlimited supply of milkshake (all flavours).

Forty per cent stake in The Kino Cinema.

Diplomatic immunity.

One grey parrot with a vocabulary of eighty-four words.

Membership to The Globe Café.

Use of the presidential carriage for domestic travel.

Use of council albatrosses (weather permitting).

Sixty-Eight Calport Avenue, Meatball District. Six bedrooms. Nine bathrooms. Paddling facilities.

Stuffed pug named Adonai.

*

The mayor called a clock toss whenever there was a slump in spirit. They invariably diverted attention and raised morale. Billions hated clocks like cockroaches. The sound of them. The shape of them. The dumb meaningless hands of them. Why would you want to be reminded of how little of something you had? They told time by the colour of the sky.

The Clock Pitch on which the tosses were held was a glistening rectangle of asphalt flanked by wooden stands. The stands were almost full when the sky spilled from raspberry to terra cotta and Casper, the mayor, and the council, rode the elevator up to the council box. They sat in deep chairs with blankets over their laps, looking down at the pitch through Perspex. Casper felt like a key being jammed into the wrong door. He tried to make out Tatiana. Where was she? He thought of his secret clock at home and wondered if he was the only person who kept one.

It began to rain.

People removed their jackets and hung them over their heads. Umbrella carriers ran to Pele and Avery, who stood at one corner of the pitch, taking it in turns to snatch a microphone from one and other. They didn't know why they were there. Their coverage was being listened to by exactly one person: their producer, on account of everyone else with a radio being in attendance.

'Wonderful idea,' Pele said, through sheets of orange rain. 'Having a clock toss to shift our attention away from nonexistent scary things! Thank you, President Captain.' He was genuinely excited and had barely noticed the drips washing his cheeks.

'Wonderful idea,' Avery said, taking back the microphone. 'Rounding us into one place to do something pointless and make us as vulnerable as possible.'

'Wonderful idea, wearing shorts when it's cold enough to see your breath.'

'I don't see any breath.'

'Because you're blind.'

'I'm not blind, they're reading glasses.'

Pele raised his fist and pumped the air. 'CLOCK TOSS,' he screamed. 'CLOCK TOSS, CLOCK TOSS, CLOCK TOSS.' Billions joined in. Soon their chant was a drumbeat loud enough to shake the rain.

Captain President pressed a button on the control panel before him and spoke. 'Good morning,' he said. 'And welcome to the nine-hundred and eighty-ninth clock toss.'

Billions hurled handfuls of popcorn and pocket lint and bellybutton fluff into the air, forming brief clouds in the wet sky above their heads. They screamed and mounted each other's shoulders. Neil Vess headbutted Ryan Vess, who toppled forward three rows and passed out in a pool of regurgitated lemonade.

The mayor coughed. 'Your first player… Daniel Hesperus.' Hesperus emerged from the tunnel dressed in a purple boiler suit and leather gloves. He faced the people and made a parting motion with his arms as though ending a magic trick.

The crowd applauded.

Their applause remained at a constant volume as President Captain introduced Mars Lipton and Elena Trotzdam, who lined up beside Hesperus on the yellow stripe that divided the court.

'And finally… Cassius Benjamin.'

The applause became so loud that Billions shot each other accusatory looks and then stopped. Cassius Benjamin bowed. President Captain continued.

'Listen, the rules are as the same as always. No schliffing, gobbing, or urinating. Interference will not be tolerated. Okay? You're okay. Begin.'

Four grandfather clocks were wheeled onto the pitch and unloaded before the four participants. They cracked their knuckles and shook their ankles and kissed their hands at the crowd.

'Daniel Hesperus,' said Daniel Hesperus.

He threw a disappointing three lions. He blamed it on an old injury sustained while cracking his sister's spine on the top bunk of a bed that collapsed as she exhaled.

'Mars Lipton.'

She threw a respectable though unimpressive six lions and pushed her entire fist into her mouth.

Casper felt something nudge his pocket. He looked down in time to see a paper caterpillar drag itself inside his trousers.

'Elena Trotzdam.'

Once unfolded, the caterpillar revealed a note from Alice.

'Cassius Benjamin.'

Diner. Dream. You're the worst.

He looked up from the note. Cassius Benjamin had thrown

ten lions. But it wasn't only the distance that people were slapping each other over. The throw had been so high that when the clock returned to earth it buried itself completely. The crowd blew bubbles.

She's going to help, Casper thought.

*

Shape landed another jump onto another rooftop. At rest, he stood like a kangaroo; hands level with his collarbones, knees bent. He looked around him. There were no columns of smoke. No patches of light. No shifting shadows.

'No time,' the voices above the clouds said. 'Go time. So tired. Always running orbits. Bed. Bed. Bed.'

He closed his eyes and listened. He heard the dim static of a distant crowd cheering. They're doing that thing they always do, he thought. Good.

Rooftops continued to scroll by beneath his feet until he glimpsed the open door of a smashed basement window and stopped. The basement window sat under a house higher than both of its neighbours combined. Its door was guarded by granite pillars. Unblemished flocks of flowers rested in planters along the entranceway.

'So much,' the voices said. 'Mornings. Mouths. Milk. So much. Too much. Blankets please, yes please. Turn it up. Way up. Sleep.'

He shimmied a drainpipe and crouched opposite Twenty-Four Ellingdon Crescent, scanning for signs of movement.

Nothing.

Usually, Shape never went inside the largest houses. Usually, the largest houses didn't have holes. Usually, everyone wasn't somewhere else.

He slid in easily, blocked the window with his coat, and clicked on his headlamp.

Piles of numbers filled the room from floor to ceiling, ending only as the walls of a thin corridor that ran between them. Shape made his way through. Numbers didn't interest him. He never took numbers. The voices above the clouds were forever talking in numbers and they were never calm or quiet.

'What?' the voices said. 'What? Listen, hear, listen. We're listening. Hello, goodbye, bedtime.'

Shape was frequently calm and quiet. On nights when the canal rose and waves beat his sandbagged hatch. When lightning made electric webs on the water. When he rifled through the things of people he didn't know, alone and undisturbed.

Shape viewed people as disturbances. Himself included. That was part of the reason for his expeditions. He had to make himself known or he wouldn't know himself.

(That was a sentence that passed through his head on a regular basis. He recognized it as meaningless and recognized meaningless as okay.)

There was nothing of interest in the kitchen. There never was. Kitchens were crucial and crucial things were the same everywhere. He bypassed all of the living rooms and went upstairs and entered the bedroom.

His hands moved directly to the bedside table. He opened a drawer and began searching.

Rings, earrings, toe rings, necklaces. Shape had enough of them already. He didn't understand people acting like mantelpieces. He only ever wore grey.

A clay board carved with letters. Three bobby pins. A pen knife.

Getting warmer.

Photographs of a dead German Shepherd. Twisted paper clips with red stains. A toucan's beak.

Who lives here? he thought, tossing aside a handmade cloth doll with Xs for eyes. Who are these people?

And then he saw it. The squirrel skull. Swaddled like a baby in blue silk. He stashed it in the pillowcase kept over his shoulder and left.

Outside, not bothering to pull himself up from ground level, Shape sprinted for an hour along narrow streets until he reached the canal. He brushed aside the lily pads that obscured his coracle, climbed in, and carefully positioned the skull between his feet.

He paddled until the sky turned tangerine and The West Wall came into view. He pushed the boat up against the floating platform on which his tent sat, got out, and tethered it to a metal loop. He pushed aside the tent flaps and unlocked the hatch that led into the canal bank.

*

The lime green tiger and me we built a tree house in the canopy of a jungle in which every tree was a birch tree and every bird was striped. An ocean of apple juice poured from a gash in the sky and the jungle filled and soon our toes were wet and our hearts were fast fast fast like scared dogs in hailstorms. On the tiger's instructions I mounted him and we set sail for a birdhouse built of peacock feathers. Our landing party was a squad of armed martens with triangles for teeth and claws sharpened to spikes. Go back, they said, no room, go back. Yes room, we shouted. Yes room. Let us come ashore. I wanted to cry. That was when the tiger knocked them all in half with one swipe and threw me onto knotted floorboards and sank beneath the waves.

*

His heartbeat was visible through his t-shirt and his wrists. He fidgeted. The diner was dark, lit by tangles of neon and a single string of fairy lights. Its blinds were kept down. People who went there didn't want to be seen there. They ate in isolated booths and spoke in hushed voices.

'Can I help you?' The waitress planted her hands on her hips. She swiped her fingers past his eyes. 'Hello?'

'Um,' he said. 'The usual.'

Her pen drumrolled the table. 'What?'

'What what?'

'I've never seen you before.'

Casper blushed. He hadn't been to The First Diner since kissing Tatiana P. Since The Dream Nurse. He hadn't noticed. The town had changed its shape since then. The Cardboard Hill hadn't. 'Do you have eels?'

'Yes.'

'Blackberries, please.'

'Mhmm.'

The waitress retreated to the kitchen as The Dream Nurse entered. She was in fur now, with a clean mouth and red blots on her cheeks. She took a seat opposite Casper. Her left hand drew a letter in the air, something the waitress recognized and noted.

'Thank you,' Casper said, not looking up.

'Why?'

'For doing this.'

'I haven't done anything.'

'Um.'

'I'm seeing you now because you put this on me. If I didn't tell you what I read and something happened to the town, it would be on me.'

'No.'

'Yes. You wouldn't have come to me if you didn't really need help. You'd be too scared.'

'Um.'

She thought he was afraid of dinosaurs. She thought he was afraid of monsters that flattened houses and choked on clouds. His chest hissed. He was afraid of the drawings on his cardboard walls remaining drawings on his cardboard walls.

'I'm not sorry for throwing my toothbrush.'

'Okay.'

Their orders arrived. Casper pushed his to one side. The Dream Nurse drank the contents of her miniature porcelain cup in one.

'Why didn't you come?' she said.

'It was too late.'

He remembered Sixteen telling him it wasn't. He remembered bed being easier, pillows getting less upset.

'It's late now. If you'd come when Sixteen pulled you out, I'd have been angry for a while and then not angry anymore.'

'I didn't know.'

'It doesn't matter. It's gone. You want to know what the dream means?'

'Please.' He felt a sudden unexpected disinterest in the dream. The words *It's gone* circled his head and dropped like a weight through his feet.

'Go ahead but go under.'

'Sorry?'

'Go ahead but go under.'

He raised his eyes for the first time. 'What does that mean?'

'I told you what the dream means. I don't know what the meaning of the dream means.'

'I don't understand.'

'Goodbye.'

'Um.'

He stared into the bundle of black ropes in his bowl. It's gone, he thought. 'What?' he asked out loud. No, it isn't. It's the opposite of gone. *Go ahead.* It was going to work. Bright, shiny Tatiana P. She was waiting at the end of this. He felt as though helium balloons had been tied to his hair.

*

Three piles of one hundred numbers each, wrapped in frayed hair ties. Six more piles to go.

Kevin was counting alone in his basement. He liked to count when things felt heavy. It was meditation and reassurance. Numbers meant safety. Enough numbers and they couldn't touch you.

His money had been made from milk. His father's father had milked cows. His father had owned cows. Kevin imported milk. All of the milk in Billion flowed through him. It wasn't glamorous money but it was solid and reliable money. Money that remained. Money that grew.

He completed another pile, bound it with a hair tie, and laid it on top of the others. Tiny money to him. Enough money to them.

As he continued, the door burst open with enough force to tip a stack of numbers, initiating a domino effect, which looked, to Kevin, like waves crashing around him.

Tatiana didn't wait for the weather to clear. She broke her way through the numbers, sat on his chest and forced her thumbs into his throat.

'What did you do with it?'

He tried to answer and managed a squawk.

'Answer me.'

His face grew translucent.

'Where?'

His lips parted like a goldfish.

'KEVIN.'

'Timeout!' said a high-pitched voice in the tone of a weather reporter announcing winter's end. A woman was fitting herself through the broken window. The woman was small. Tatiana put her at four and a quarter. The woman was wearing an oversized t-shirt as a dress, revealing collarbones that stuck out like tents.

'What are you doing in my house, you—'

'I thought it was the milkman's house, grumpy. Only he doesn't seem to be answering the door.'

She took slow, certain steps forward. Tatiana relaxed her grip on Kevin and he rolled out from under her. 'Get out.'

'Are you going to wrestle me too? I should warn you, I don't have any interest in climbing inside your nose, so it may prove difficult.'

'Who are you?'

The woman curtseyed. 'Kimya Cole,' she said. 'I know, right?' Tatiana didn't have time to respond, although her eyes did, as the woman struck her in the temple with two fingers, and she collapsed unconscious on the fallen numbers. 'May she rest in peace,' Kimya Cole said.

'What?'

'Joking.'

The two of them stared at the body, now rendered harmless, limbs spread out at unnatural angles like broken wings.

'You shouldn't have done that.'

'No problem.'

'Please leave.'

'Night night, milkman.'

Kimya Cole hopped through the window and disappeared into the pistachio green. Kevin took rapid breaths until his shaking ceased. He raked numbers over Tatiana's legs and chest, then finished counting out the bundles and stowed them in a rucksack. He left the house and made for the closest watchtower. Black thumbprints made themselves known on his throat.

*

Dinner was leek sausages and peas and mashed potato. Sixteen cooked the sausages. Diana made the vegetables. She carried them to the table he had laid and sat down beside him and they ate.

After filling her stomach halfway, she set down her spoon and patted her belly.

'That was a good one,' she said.

'You're finished?'

'No, the clock toss.'

'Sure.'

'Casper was in the council box.'

'I know.'

'I think it's nice he's got something to occupy himself with.'

Sixteen frowned and swallowed. 'You'd rather have him fight dinosaurs than be bored?'

'Not bored, lazy.'

'Can we not talk about him? We talk about him more than we talk about us.'

'There's nothing wrong with us.'

'I haven't emptied in three days.'

'Not at the table.' She folded her arms. He resumed eating. 'You really think I think that?'

'I really think you think what?'

'You think I think it's better that he's in danger than if he's moping around?'

'I only asked.'

'You weren't really asking. You were telling.'

'What do you want me to say?'

'I don't know.'

She left the table. He finished his meal, bound hers in cling film, and fell asleep to a person in the radio listing edible fungi.

*

Casper couldn't face the milk bar. The clock toss was enough. The Dream Nurse was enough. He was drinking in The Queen's. The only two people who were ever there never asked him about dinosaurs or talked in horrified excitement about the night and its overdue arrival. They didn't know Tatiana P or Cassius Benjamin. They had other concerns, outside of The Circle, away from the people who lifted him onto their shoulders.

Cerulean light filtered through the fogged windows. Ned Kloot was playing pachinko. Casper and the barman were playing a drinking game in which each participant took turns to name a fear and those who suffered from it drank.

'Ghosts,' the barman said.

Neither of them moved.

'Lions,' Casper said.

The barman drank.

'Not lions?'

Casper shrugged. 'They're always sweet when I dream.'

'The West Wall.'

They both drank.

'The Jungle.'

They both drank.

'Ella Peti.'

'I don't know who that is.'

'Be grateful,' the barman said, drinking deeply.

'Sand,' Casper said.

The barman wrinkled his nose.

'I'm running out of things.'

'Leaving nothing behind,' the barman said.

They both drank. Ned Kloot turned to them and grinned. He poured his milk out onto the floor.

'Drainpipes,' he said. 'I've got more pachinko balls than my house can hold.'

'Okay, Ned, thank you. I think it's time to close.'

'One more game,' Ned said, stooping to the carpet for his lost milk.

'No more games.'

'You're the worst.'

'I know.'

Casper paid, pulled on his jacket, and left. Sleepy pairs of people making their ways home from bars were staggered along the street. He kept his face hidden, hurrying in a way that he hoped would arouse no suspicion. The train was still running and the cold encouraged him to take it. It was too risky though. Alleyways were safer. The train was a hive of people too scared to take dark paths.

It took a full sky change to reach the shipping container. It lay beyond almost everything, in what had once been a dock and was now a junkyard of ship hulls and rusted anchors. He saw only one person once he had left the circle; a mechanic carrying a plastic pedal back to his shop. They did not acknowledge each other.

George Stanza swung open the container door as soon as Casper knocked. 'You didn't ask me the password. I told you to ask me the password.'

'Sorry, Casper.'

'Ask me now.'

'Yes.'

Casper said nothing else. He knew that whatever anger he felt was misplaced. He should be the one saying sorry. Sorry, sorry, sorry. *I am the worst person in the world and I need your help.*

He delivered his instructions standing up, while George sat on the bed, making manic motions with his hands. What is he doing? Casper thought. Is he mocking me?

'Go ahead but under,' he concluded. George grinned, floundered to the floor, and dragged himself under the bed. 'What are you doing? Come out.'

George Stanza reemerged. He very slowly invited to Casper to eat with him and Casper very quickly declined.

'Good luck,' he said.

'Sorry, Casper.'

It was late enough for the train to be less of a danger. The only other passenger was a one-eyed girl with racks of sticks balanced on her shoulders. She smiled. He examined the space between his feet.

The receptionist at Hotel Ponzi attempted to engage Casper in conversation. He collected his key and said nothing. He stood in the elevator and said nothing. He went into his room and spun the bath taps, undressing and sitting on the lip of the tub with his feet in the water as it filled. Steam blocked out the walls and he imagined himself to be somewhere else, somewhere in the past, where everything was set and solid and confined within cardboard.

Tentatively lowering himself into the water, he thought of The Dream Nurse.

She never used to be The Dream Nurse. She used to be Alice. She used to call him ant baby and feed him grilled worms.

He let himself sink.

Bubbles engulfed his face.

Her face evaporated to be replaced with images of Tatiana. Tatiana calling him down from the rooftops. Tatiana's wonky fortuneteller predicting hail. He pictured Kevin's rough hands stapled to her sides. His fat finger forcing its way through her nose and out the back of her skull. When he climbed out of the bath, there were holes in his palms where his nails had buried themselves.

The bed was cold and foreign. He fell in and rolled to one side, leaving behind a damp silhouette. He felt guilty. He was guilty. He was a sinkhole dragging people into the unknown.

*

Dinosaurs have traditionally been thought to herald the arrival of the night. Relentless, gnashing monsters, sent by the voices above the clouds to clear our town for their arrival. Bulldozers for the unseen. Agents of the darkness.

It is generally accepted that they are malicious beings to be feared and dominated, so as to prevent their taking over of the town. Interestingly, it has not always been seen this way.

Alfred Font, grandfather of Crispin the Great, held a different, and widely disputed, view. He posited that they were tests. Tests constructed by the unseen in order to ascertain whether or not we were prepared for our ascent. He maintained that it was his duty to slay every one of them in order to prove himself worthy of being called up beyond the clouds.

Alfred Font's remains were discovered in a deep corner of The Jungle by a gem miner. They were decaying in a decrepit wooden house built into the crown of a redwood tree.

A,

I stopped thinking about the window height. I had visitors. First, Leti came. We drank. We didn't sleep. We woke a drug dealer up four times. We sat in the bath. She asked me if I'd put a baby in her. I said no. I said it would jump out of a window before it could talk. In the morning, we decide to become addicted to heroin. We couldn't find any heroin. One person she called started screaming. Saying he was coming over right now to tie her up and beat it out of her. I started vomiting. She left. Next, another girl came. I'd met her once before. She liked my books. She called. I told her I was in the hotel. And asked her to bring wine. And we kissed. Slept. Kissed. Slept. Kissed. Slept. Just like that.

When she left I met the Russian couple across the hall. They couldn't make their room key fit. He was small. She was blonde. They cooked food and we ate and drank vodka. I don't remember what we talked about. But I know we talked a lot. And loudly. It felt like being cured of something heavy. I thought about Vonnegut. And being in a Karass. Everything seemed a bit better. And like it was time to go.

Pedro said I couldn't go. Not like that. The last few weeks were bad. It would be better to end on something else. So we had a party. A goodbye party. I wrote a chapbook to give away. We made speeches about how much we liked each other. More people than could fit in the bar turned up. It was fun.

I'm leaving in the morning. It's sad to leave. It's so hot here. Houses are probably falling into the sea at home. I'm on Pedro's sofa, with their white poodle dozing on my chest. The sky's almost gone,

C

Three.

Pele woke up hungry in the ninth largest villa in Billion. He drew back the curtains of his bed, wincing as fuchsia light hit his eyes. The bedroom was filled with untouched furniture and polished lumps of brass. Oil paintings on the walls depicted basset hounds clumsily engaging in various human sports.

He tied the cord of his dressing gown and went downstairs.

The fridge was bare. The cupboards were bare. He checked his washing machine and it was bare.

Assuming that the streets would be barren, he left the house in what he was wearing and headed for the bakery on Fifth Street. He'd get what he always got; two sesame seed rolls and four slices of ham. He'd eat it with the radio on. He'd shower. After that, he'd bring a litre of the best banana milk to Avery and apologise and agree to play along with *the night is coming* until everyone got bored of it.

Rounding a corner by the aquarium, he saw something he'd always believed no one would ever see.

The T-Rexasaurus was swaying as though sleepwalking. Its glass-loaded jaw swallowed air as its undersized arms pedaled mechanically. It looked lost, like some alien creature dropped from a passing plane.

Pele froze, not breathing.

His first thought was of Avery and how they'd fought and how that would be their ending.

His second thought was of his house and how it was empty and how it would soon be someone else's.

His third thought concerned the tearing of flesh from his body and how much it would hurt and how soon it would be over.

The T-Rexasaurus failed to pause. It continued to wobble dumbly away.

Pele waited until he could no longer see it to open his mouth. He had to plead with his legs to start working. He asked them and then he asked them nicely. They complied and broke into a run, stopping only on the floor of his living room, where he unzipped a rucksack and proceeded to fill it with numbers, blankets, clothes, knives, and bottled milk from his cellar.

He had to leave. He had to go somewhere. Anywhere. If the dinosaurs were there then the night was coming and he knew nothing. The map he'd made in his head was wrong. He could be tugged from his house at any minute. He needed to go. Now.

The first train to arrive at the station was going in the opposite direction of the dinosaur. He climbed aboard, lifted his pack onto his lap, and sank his face into it. The train chugged through the morning until it terminated at the tearoom by the canal.

*

George Stanza made his way uncertainly towards the place that Casper had ordered him to, using a map written on a milk mat, held awkwardly inside the ribcage of his costume. The spot was a building beside a bridge over the dry stream. Once there, he pressed his back to a wall and waited.

He tried not to think about the potential for failure. House, he thought. Numbers. People. House.

His target came into view. She was a platinum girl with legs that looked as though they should end in paws. Hello, he thought. She had her back to him. He coughed then remembered what he was supposed to be. He wailed. She turned and froze.

'Argh,' George screamed again, hoping that it sounded dinosaur-like and not being convinced that it did.

'Argh,' Tatiana screamed back.

'Argh.'

'Argh.'

This is boring, thought George.

'Argh.'

'Argh.'

Where is he? thought George. He said he'd be right here.

He said I wouldn't have to keep her occupied. I don't know how to be a dinosaur. I'm not a dinosaur.

It was then that he heard loud footsteps clapping the pavement behind him.

*

Kevin had slept outside, under the statue of Crispin the Great. He chose the statue partly because it was central yet rarely busy, and partly because Crispin the Great was Casper's great-grandfather. Crispin Font had been the most revered and prolific dinosaur hunter in Billion. Allegedly, the number of dinosaurs he had killed was higher than the number of words he knew. After him, the Fonts no longer had any purpose. There were no more dinosaurs. Crispin spent his last days motionless in bed, a radio at his head and boiled sweets in his hands. Each successive son moved farther and farther out of town, as their numbers dwindled and they became forgotten.

Until now.

Kevin wouldn't let it happen. Killing the T-Rexasaurus would be easy. It was a thing that moved and all moving things could be stopped if you hit them hard enough.

He was woken by a firm shake. The watchman wanted the rest of his money. Kevin obliged. He drew himself into a sitting position, splashed his face with bottled water, and beat his left hand with the bat clasped in his right. The watchman pointed toward a bridge that intersected Tatiana's jogging route.

'Thank you.'

'Whatever.'

Kevin walked and the future played out inside his head.

Maybe she'll be there, he thought. Maybe she'll witness my victory firsthand. I'll run bloody hands through her hair. She'll wrap her legs around my waist. I'll lift her. I'll throw her through the sky and catch her on my back. We'll be the richest couple in

Billion. I'll become mayor. The people will want that. A mayor who can keep them safe. A mayor with thick arms and a lump of coal where his fears and doubts should be. A mayor who can straddle the night, pin it to the ground and force out of it a promise never to return.

*

When the news reached Casper, he vaulted the hotel balcony and sprinted, in his underwear, to the bridge over the dry stream. Several Billions were uncertainly circling the scene, wanting good vantage points as well as safety.

The scene: A bat wielding Kevin, looming over the T-Rexasaurus, which had slumped to the ground, its stubby arms uselessly flailing.

'Stop,' Casper shouted.

'No,' Kevin replied. 'You've lost.' Tatiana, now safely stood with the other Billions, felt a flash of weird pride.

He brought the bat down on the dinosaur's head. The dinosaur's head fell away from the dinosaur's body.

There was a brief moment of silence.

Then a violent wailing, launched from the mouth of George Stanza's floating face. Kevin looked to Casper, then to his victim, then back to Casper. It didn't make sense. What was happening?

The cry grew in intensity as George struggled in the suit, thrashing and twisting, the dent in his skull throbbing like a heart.

More Billions materialized.

'Someone help him.'

'It's a trick!'

'No one help him.'

'How is it a trick?'

'Does anyone else feel like super bad about this?'

Casper stepped toward George as Kevin stepped toward Casper, arms stiff out ahead like a zombie. They collided and fell.

'STOP,' a voice from above ordered. It was louder than anything anyone could remember. 'What have you done?'

A hand the size of a house knocked aside clouds and gripped George Stanza by the collar, towing him up. As he rose, Tatiana clapped and bounced. As he rose, he hollered. 'I'm not the one. Casper's the one. He made me do it. I'm not the one. Let me down. Let me go. Let me down.'

*

Things said by the bridge over the dry stream in the immediate wake of Casper Font's arrest:

Diana to Dr Sixteen: You are never seeing him again.

Dr Sixteen to Diana: nothing.

Kevin to Tatiana: I did it.

Tatiana to Kevin: Struck the slowest person in Billion.

Neil Vess to Kimya Cole: Kevin is the worst person ever in the whole town ever.

Kimya Cole to Ryan Vess: We are all in battles.

Ryan Vess to Kimya Cole: I like your hair. Who are you? What was that hand?

Angelica to no one: Where are the penguins?

The mayor to everyone: BE CALM. GO HOME. THERE ARE NO DINOSAURS. YOU ARE NOT IN DANGER.

*

'You're listening to Nine FM with Keira Mary-Kate. The sky is currently magenta and the cloud count is… we don't know. Look up. It doesn't matter.

In a dramatic turn of events, it was today revealed that the threat of dinosaurs was in fact a hoax, allegedly engineered by the great grandson of Crispin the Great, Casper Font, of The Cardboard Hill, Little Poland. It is believed that he created the dinosaur, which was in fact no more than a person in a suit, in order to con the town of Billion out of numbers and achieve for himself a level of status similar to that of his ancestors. Had his plan succeeded, Font's reward, which included a property in The Meatball District and shares in The Kino Cinema, would have made him the wealthiest man in Billion.

The standoff ended dramatically, with an unidentified hand emerging from the sky and stealing away a person who has yet to be identified. Some have claimed that this is verification for the existence of the voices above the clouds. Others have said that it was a trick of the light and everyone at the scene had drunk too much milk.

We go now to Milo Almond, who's live outside the Mayor's office. Milo?'

'Thank you, Keira. I'm live outside the Mayor's office. There are loads of people here and stuff. Someone said they're having a council meeting in there, I think. They're going to decide what to do next, I guess.'

'Could you describe the mood of the crowd?'

'Someone just jumped onto my back and yelled at me to 'giddyup.' Everyone is eating popcorn. I can see a human pyramid. Everyone is kind of happy and kind of sad.'

'What are people saying about the hand?'

'That it's... really weird and kind of scary.'

'Could you be more specific?'

'Not really, no. And I don't understand why I've been sent here. I told you, I can't do this job. This isn't my job.'

'Stop being pathetic.'

'Leave me alone.'

'And back to the studio, with me, Keira Mary-Kate. Now time for an update on the scandal, with Avery Vitafit.'

'Does this smell like Earl Grey to you? Really? Shall we rinse you with it and find out?'

'Avery?'

'Get out, you doghole. Get out and try again. Try harder. Try your hardest and maybe someone somewhere will be proud.'

'Avery?'

'Shut up, Kiera, I can hear you. Not much else happened. The mayor refused to comment. One of his council, Paul Linklater, said that he 'objected' to what had happened today. Nothing about the hand. There's going to be a trial. Tomorrow. Tangerine.'

'Thank you for the update. You've been listening to Nine FM with me, Keira Mary-Kate. The sky is still magenta. There are no dinosaurs.'

Avery hung up his headphones and moved through to the adjacent lounge where his wife sat, sipping weak tea and half-heartedly colouring in a line drawing of a cheetah. She'd told him she'd come to stop him from 'doing anything stupid', though they both saw the excuse as transparent. Avery never did 'anything stupid.' He made sometimes mistakes. It was different. It was tripping on rocks, not diving into concrete.

'Ready?'

'Yes.'

They held hands and descended the stairs. Avery had been to Pele's villa that morning. He had brought breakfast rolls and a thermos of tea. Pele hadn't been there. The bottled water, knives, and rucksack hadn't been there either. Pele hadn't been at the bakery. Pele hadn't been at the studio where they'd been scheduled to arrive when the sky flipped. Avery knew there must be some connection with the pretend dinosaur. He had no idea what the connection might be.

*

President Captain had not yet held a meeting of the council. He was embarrassed to face them because he blamed himself and he didn't want to face them because he blamed them all.

Instead, he was eating Battenberg with his wife and intermittently tearing up.

'I don't understand,' he said. 'He tried refusing every gift we offered. Why would he do this?'

Lucille drew comforting circles on his back with her palm. 'It doesn't matter. It's over.'

'It's not over. I look weak. I look stupid.'

'You look like a lion.'

'Would a lion do this?' He fell to his knees, hung his tongue out from the corner of his mouth, and waddled five paces forward, making seal-like sounds.

'They're not against you,' she said.

He stood up and strode to the window, parting the curtain with his fingers and wincing at the crowd assembled below. 'Aren't they?'

'They're against him. You need to show them that you're on their side.' Lucille Captain always tried her hardest to aid her husband. Her forehead was at stake. She touched it with her palm and shuddered. She wondered if tonight would require a helmet.

'The trial,' her husband said, straightening himself. 'I'll sentence him to execution.'

'Can you do that?'

'I don't know.' President Captain slumped. 'Probably not.'

'You can put him in jail until forever.'

'I hope so.'

Deaf Paul wandered into the room, obliviously mumbling and swatting invisible flies with his giant hands. The mayor screamed. There was no response. He gripped Deaf Paul by the waist and drove him out of the room. Deaf Paul didn't resist.

'He doesn't know any better,' Lucille said, locking the door. 'It's not his fault.'

*

The IV drip leaked nutritional formula into Alec Cole's blood. Kimya sat on the floor by his bed, watching the bag empty. It was becoming increasingly difficult to remember him how he had been. Before he stopped moving.

Giving speeches from the balcony. Opening his arms like a funnel for the rain. Telling them to meet him on the roof. She whispered to him about the hand.

'We're being looked after,' she said. 'They are up there. It's okay. Sleep.'

*

The tearoom on the canal was six storeys high and timber framed, with sheets of glass for walls. There was no electricity. Mangled candles sat on the driftwood tables. Pele Marti sat, looking across the canal, at the fringes of The Jungle on the other side. Raspberry light fell through the trees and spelled patterns on the dirt. Further in, there was only black.

Pele had heard a lot of things about The Jungle. Everyone knew stories. Polar bears that wore blood as lipstick. Deranged tribes of fur covered people. The last dinosaurs. Avery had once told him that no one who went in, completely in, ever came out. Pele had laughed.

Now The Jungle seemed the best place to hide. Clearly the dinosaurs weren't there. They were in the town. He would build himself a treehouse and learn to hunt. He would bang a rock with a stick and make fire. He would wear coats made of leaves and sleep on beds of moss.

'Excuse me,' he said, calling over the waitress. The waitress was named Eliza Seuss. The tearoom had been her inheritance. It was forever empty and she was forever dreaming about moving into the town, taking a job in the mayor's office and swimming in the mornings after continental buffet breakfasts. 'Do you rent boats?'

'You are crossing?'

'Yes, to The Jungle.'

The majority of her customers were Billions who chose to do this. They invariably failed to return. For this reason, the deposits were extremely high. She didn't know what was in The Jungle. She guessed monsters.

'Follow me.'

They made their way down the tearoom with the aid of a gas lamp, until they came to a dark chamber beneath the bottom floor in which a stable of canoes were roped together, bobbing on the black water. He gave her the fee and the deposit, stowed his bag at the back of the nearest vessel, then climbed in and paddled out from under the building.

He had planned to simply row across the canal, dump the boat, and enter The Jungle, but being on the water felt calming. Nothing could reach him there. He was a moated castle. Dinosaurs couldn't swim.

He continued on, away from the town, toward places that he didn't know. Maybe there are other towns, he thought. Safer towns, with higher walls. Do we even have walls? He thought of Avery and rowed so hard his arms felt like bursting at the seams.

*

Casper had only been in the holding cell for one sky change and had already invented several new games. *How many ceiling tiles? How many scratches before the skin breaks? Toenail trimming with teeth. Spitting on your feet while in a headstand.* He was trying to avoid thinking about things it was no longer productive to think about.

The holding cell consisted of a splintered wooden floor, a thin mattress, a tin potty, and one blanket. A metal hatch in the door afforded him a view of a brick wall and a guard named Jean Ralphio, who spent most of his time practicing ballet positions in front of a mirror he'd brought himself. He had particular trouble with fifth. Casper had tried to engage him in conversation and he'd replied with a zipping motion across his lips and a wonky pirouette.

Casper unfolded the blanket, lay at one end of it, and rolled, wrapping himself up in a cocoon. A fist beat the door.

'Visitor,' the guard called. Casper fought with the blanket as Dr Sixteen stepped in and sat down.

'Having trouble?'

'No.'

Sixteen looked gaunt and anxious. His shoes were odd. He removed a packet of wine gums from his coat, tore them open, and offered one to his friend. The two of them sat, loudly chewing, taking in where they'd found themselves.

'How did it look?' Casper asked.

'Better than I expected.'

'What are they saying?'

'Some people don't think you knew. I don't know why. Some people think you made the people in the clouds angry, and now we're going to pay.'

'The night thing.'

'Yes, the night thing.'

'People really think the night is coming?'

'A massive hand came out of the sky. Of course they think the night is coming. And people always thought that, you just didn't notice. Only now they think it even more.'

'What do you think?'

'I think this trial is going to go badly.'

Casper hadn't thought at all about the trial. He assumed there would be one, but that it would be a formality. At this stage, there was no way he could extricate himself from what had happened. He had motive and means and there was damning evidence in the form of George Stanza's final words.

'The trial is pointless.'

'I'll be acting as your lawyer.'

Casper forced a smile. 'Thank you. Don't bother. I've already lost. It will only get you in trouble with Diana.'

'I'm in trouble already. You made the whole town petrified so that you could climb closer to the scariest girl this side of The Jungle.'

'Have they told you anything about it?'

'Not really. It will happen tomorrow. Tangerine. Someone called Sligo is going to be making the case against you.'

'Sligo?'

'Apparently.'

Casper flicked a wine gum into the air and caught it in his mouth. 'What will they do to me?'

'Jail. For a long time. Probably.'

'That's not too bad.'

'You don't know who else is in there.'

'Who else is in there?'

'No one.'

Dr Sixteen got to his feet. 'Wait,' Casper said. 'Help me escape.'

'How?'

'Bring me a set of Diana's clothes and a crate of toilet paper.'

'See you tomorrow.'

'Alright.'

Sixteen left the holding cell feeling three times his normal weight. He had a shift at The Doll Hospital to complete and the trial to prepare for. Diana had expressly forbidden him from participating. She was going to throw things when she found out. She was going to turn into a beetroot and disown him.

*

Kelis Vitafit considered her husband to be a ship that had recently landed on the ocean floor. They had searched everywhere and found nothing. Now, Avery was refusing to get out of bed. He was catatonic. She had liked Pele, but felt this to be an overreaction. She thought he was probably unconscious somewhere, or lost, or looking for something. She didn't think it was connected to the hand. She thought the hand was an elaborate practical joke put on by someone from The Circle who was rich and bored.

'Time for the studio,' she said, rapping her husband with a bamboo cane she'd found under the stairs. 'Get up.'

He didn't move. She went into the bathroom and climbed into the bathtub. Was she really not enough to even bother moving for? I should leave, she thought. I shouldn't stay here, being transparent and whatnot. If he continues his surrender, the villa will be taken away anyway. The producer will turn up and break down the door. He'll dismantle the walls and carry everything away.

The producer.

She had an idea. She'd go to the studio in Avery's place. She'd put out a call asking for information regarding Pele's whereabouts. When a reliable tip-off came in, she'd relay it to her husband and he'd be forced to get out of bed and search for his friend. That's what he needs, she thought. He needs to do more.

*

Tatiana P alternated between beating Kevin, laughing hysterically at him, and contemplating Kimya Cole while binge eating biscuits alone in the attic. She pushed a bourbon into her mouth whole. A blanket was draped over her head.

She hadn't been attacked before. There weren't many people in Billion capable of landing punches and so, being one herself, it was unlikely she'd come across another.

She knew who Kimya Cole was. Kimya Cole was the sister of the last mayor. Alec Cole. She'd lived with Alec Cole until she didn't want to live with Alec Cole anymore.

A burning pain stung her calf. She rolled up the leg of her one piece pyjama suit and found a black umbrella. She shook the blanket from her head and applauded the sky. It was time.

*

Anonymous tip offs received concerning the whereabouts of Pele Marti following Kelis Vitafit's appeal on Nine FM:

'He's in my hole.'

'He was totally obviously the person in the dinosaur. The hand took him. He should feel lucky he got carried up like that. If he hadn't, I would have stuffed his throat with paper and set him on fire myself.'

'He's burning numbers in The Kissing Hall.'

'B, Calamari.'

'Definitely not.'

'There's a guy by the aviary, dressed in toilet paper, pretending to be an elephant. I think it might be him. In fact, I'm certain it's him.'

'I saw him with an orange rucksack on a train headed for the tearoom by the canal.'

*

The faint clouds of a mint green sky were reflected in the water of the canal. Shape rowed slowly, grinning at the stillness as he tried to decide on corners in The Burrow for his new possessions. It had been a productive day. He'd acquired a peacock feather, three milk teeth, a fez, some kind of wooden catapult, and an ostrich egg. It had been a strong day in some respects and an unsuccessful day in others.

Some time ago, Shape had entered a house and filled his sack with porcelain figurines from a sea chest in the bedroom. Downstairs, he'd found another team of figures that appealed to him significantly more than the first. Only, it didn't make sense to empty his load and refill. And when whoever lived there realized they'd been robbed, they'd likely be more careful with their belongings. He climbed the kitchen and hid the figures on top of the tallest cabinet, a cabinet so tall that only a finger length sat between it and the ceiling. He was confident the person would consider these figures stolen too, allowing him to return and steal them for real.

Only now he couldn't find the house again. He'd left hastily, startled by the dream screams of its occupant, a girl calling out for a person that was no longer there.

How hard could it be to get back to somewhere he'd already been?

He sighed as he tethered his boat to the wooden platform and unloaded his cargo. He pushed aside the flap and entered. He paused. He turned around and went back outside.

Another boat. One of the teahouse canoes.

He wasn't expecting anyone.

The Burrow's entrance was not at all disguised and it had never occurred to Shape to try. He never suffered visitors. Billions were too scared of The West Wall. They knew Something must lie on the other side of it and they had no idea what the Something could be. They were scared of the unknown. They always saw monsters in the darkness. Shape never did. He sometimes considered himself to be a monster. Not a particularly malevolent one, just one that swum through people's lives, poking holes when their backs were turned.

He stepped into the antechamber. A giant hall covered with stolen watercolour paintings. Shape had a penchant for paintings of trees in winter, specifically birch trees, specifically birch trees with frowning faces scratched into their silver trunks.

Various tunnels led out of the antechamber and to his bedroom, bathroom, lounge, kitchen, and several storage halls, or 'galleries.' He didn't want to startle his guest. He wanted to observe his guest, and ascertain whether or not his guest would pose a threat or something quieter, softer, and rounder at the edges.

Pele was in the third storage hall.

Pele looked like a newborn baby. He was curled tightly, with a thumb in his mouth and both of his shoes untied. Either side of him stood tangled piles of brass lamps, stuffed capybaras, and wedding veils.

Shape clapped.

Pele opened his eyes, sleepily and fractionally at first, then wide, and all at once. He jumped to his feet and leapt to one side, falling through an ongoing project Shape referred to as The Pyramid of Teeth.

'Who is this?' Shape said, tilting his head.

Pele scrambled backwards. 'Get away.' He groped the mound of objects to his side, settling on a silver candelabra and pitching it at Shape's head.

Shape ducked and grinned. 'What you do this for?'

'I don't know. To stop you from killing me.'

Shape held his belly and laughed. 'Why?'

'I don't want to die.'

'I am not going to killing you.'

Pele visibly relaxed, then tensed again, suspicious. 'Why not?'

'You want this?'

'No. Please don't. Please.'

'If you are insisting.' He sat down and took a block of fudge from his pocket, breaking it into halves and passing one to his visitor. Pele stared at his block and waited for Shape to take a bite before he did. It had quickly become apparent that he hadn't brought enough food. Pele was a comfort eater. His time in The Burrow so far had been mainly spent imagining dinosaurs and black forest gateau.

'Shape,' said Shape. He pointed at Pele between the eyes. 'Who is this?'

'Shape who called in to the show?'

'You are laughing radio man?'

'I'm sorry.'

'Okay, now I kill you.'

'Please, I'm sorry.'

'I joke.'

'Okay.'

They paused.

'You must go,' Shape said. Pele stood. 'You may stay.' Pele sat. 'You must leave right now this minute.' Pele stood. 'You sit, you stay.' He wanted to check. Fraternizing meant a loss of control. He didn't know what to do. 'I do hear them, you must know this. They are up there.'

Neither of them said anything. Shape supposed there was only one reason a radio presenter would flee a town that had given him everything he could hold. 'It is beginning, no?'

'What?'

'You can stay.'

They ate without talking. When they were done, Shape left the chamber for his bedroom. Pele moulded a nest from bridal veils and wondered whether or not he was supposed to be afraid.

A,

I'm in the air now. Drinking wine. Eating peanuts. Thinking about hijacking the plane. Crashing it into something big. And with lots of people inside. Well-liked people, with large families, and responsibilities. People who will be missed.

Don't worry. I'm not going to do it. I always think about the worst possible thing I could do in any situation. So I get to feel proud about not doing it. During exams in school I thought about standing up and undressing and shouting racist things. You probably remember that I never did.

The woman next to me is eating her fingernails. She looks like a terrapin but smells like warm rhubarb. I think it's a waste of time we're not together in the toilet. She's eating her fingernails. I'm emailing you. We're the best thing each other could be doing. And we're not doing it. People never are. It's very boring. I think I might be drunk. Or almost.

I just asked for more wine. The hostess gave me red. I can't drink red wine. It takes too long. Also it's the colour of the blood that comes up when you're sick. Vomit blood is darker than papercut blood. My favourite t-shirt has lots of Ribena blots.

I'm worried these emails seem selfish. Because I don't ask you questions. I only talk about myself. It's because you don't reply. It feels like talking to a pet. If you did reply, there are a lot of things I would ask you.

Do you still believe in ghosts? Do you participate in sporting activities? Do you watch any? If yes, do you shout at your television and throw things and is your mood immediately afterwards dependent on the result? Are you taller than average? Can you juggle? Do you ever wake up in the night and go outside to smoke and wish that an as yet unidentified species of monster would appear and eat you? Are you vegan? Do you have pets? How many words do you think you know? Do you foresee your current relationship ending at some point in the future? What do you predict will cause the end? Do you think the world will end within your lifetime? If yes, do you think it will end because of aliens, meteors, global warming, a global epidemic of depression, nuclear whatever, or something else? What do you eat when you're hungover? Which writers make you feel less alone?

Sorry. That's a lot of questions. I don't have anything to do but type at you. I tried to write. But I have to drink a lot before I think I have things to say. That's why I'm quiet in public. I'm not empty, just unconvinced,

C

Four.

Billions:
 The trial of Casper Font
 and an official statement
 concerning the hand
 that broke through the sky.
 The Courtroom.
 Not mandatory.
 Tangerine.
 Be Calm.

*

On the morning of the trial, Casper woke up with a dead leg, Sixteen woke up in an empty bed, Shape didn't sleep at all, Pele dreamed of countries where they wrote in symbols, and Avery was shaken awake by his wife. She told him that his friend had been seen heading to the tearoom on the canal. They sat side by side on the edge of the bed with their hands in each other's laps. They guessed he was scared. That he would hide himself in the jungle. They guessed that his paper castle had been set alight.

*

'Put this on,' Dr Sixteen said, dropping a pressed navy suit onto Casper. 'And comb your hair.'

'I don't have a comb.'

'Come here.' Sixteen spat onto his hands and clapped them on Casper's head, flattening the pyramids of hair stuck up by restless sleep.

When Casper had changed out of his clothes, they stood facing each other, hands on each other's shoulders. 'We can do this, I think.'

'What are we going to say?'

'We're going to say that you didn't know. That George had
a vendetta against you and he used the opportunity to knock
you down a deep hole.'

'George didn't have vendettas.'

'What else do you want to say?'

'Tatiana.'

'Stop it.'

Casper sunk into a pile on the bare floor, beating his knuckles against the stone. He was confused about what his head was
saying. His head was saying Tatiana, over and over, in the voice
of a child divorced from its parents.

*

President Captain blinked. He located his wife in the crowd.
A world map painted in beetroot crossed her forehead. He
looked at the notes on his podium. His notes said three things:

-Don't look scared.

-Don't wet yourself.

-Burn the Dinosaur Hunter.

The courtroom felt bigger than he could remember it ever
feeling. Its dark wooden panels seemed to close in and jump
apart like elevator doors. They looked to be burning in the tangerine light. Last time he'd been passing a verdict, the charges
had concerned accidental destruction of property during The
Tentacle Festival. The defence made jokes. The audience bel-
lowed as though they were at a clock toss. Handfuls of shredded
toilet paper littered the air.

This time, everyone was silent.

They blinked back at him like newborn babies.

He tried to speak and choked on a ball of cotton. Lucille
Captain nodded. 'Good morning,' he said. 'I know you're all
scared and I'm sorry.' He wanted to signal to the sound engineer
and shrink his voice to nothing. He wanted to climb beneath the

stage like he had when he'd first become mayor. 'We have The Dinosaur Hunter and we're going to throw him away.'

The mayor had expected applause. There was none. His wife covered her mouth with her palms.

'What about the hand?' Kevin shouted.

'What about the penguins?' Angelica screamed.

'No one cares about the penguins.'

'The hand,' he said. 'Is nothing.'

Billions erupted into deafening unrest.

Waiting in the wing, Sixteen smiled at Casper. The people didn't care about the fake dinosaur. They cared about the hand. They cared about the night and about disappearing and about still having toffee for breakfast on mornings when it was too cold to leave bed.

President Captain said silence and then he said it again and then he screamed it. Nothing happened. He signaled at the sound engineer to turn the volume up to maximum and he punched the microphone. A giant whomp made people force their hands to their ears.

'Bring out Casper Font,' said the mayor.

Casper and Dr Sixteen were escorted from the wing by Elgar and Kismet. Casper was led to the box and Sixteen stood beside Sligo in the front row, wishing he'd bought a briefcase or some other kind of formidable looking home for paper.

Sligo wore a raincoat, fingerless gloves, and was barefooted. His pockets were filled with bottle tops.

'We are here today,' the mayor said. 'Because it looks like Casper Font probably forced George Stanza to play a dinosaur, in order to kill it and become the richest the man in Billion.'

'That's not why I did it.'

'Why did you do it?'

Casper stared through Tatiana P and said nothing.

'I'll take it from here,' said Sligo, rising. His voice was like syrup running through a copper pipe. 'Mr Font, why do you think your own financial gain should take priority over the mental wellbeing of the entire city?'

'Objection,' said Sixteen, slapping Sligo.

'Stop it,' said the mayor. 'We changed that rule. You can just say it now. No hitting.'

'Sorry, I didn't know.'

'Answer my question.'

'Don't answer his question, it's a stupid question. Answer this question: did you know George Stanza planned to dress up as a dinosaur and run about making people scared and so on?'

'I didn't know that.'

'Didn't you?' asked Sligo, flicking a binder containing pencil drawings of whales onto the floor. 'This file says otherwise.'

'Let me see that,' said the mayor. It was brought to him. He turned through it, sporadically nodding and thumbing his chin. 'That's exactly what this says.'

'It could say anything. It could say pigs ate clouds if it wanted to.' Sixteen wagged his fists. 'Who even wrote it? There's no evidence to support Casper's involvement, apart from George Stanza saying whatever he said when he was taken away. George Stanza only said that because he wanted Casper to be locked up because he tried to put his finger in Casper's nose and Casper hit him with a wrench.'

'Casper Font, is this true?'

'I guess so.'

The courtroom murmured. They didn't much care. They were shifting onto his side. Kissing drama was more exciting than much else.

*

Deaf Paul was the first Billion to see a real dinosaur. He didn't go to the trial. He hadn't heard about it. He had been out wading through the rice terraces and was returning to The Circle

via a network of abandoned streets that had long been out-
grown.

The real T-Rexasaurus was significantly larger, louder, and
more confident than George Stanza. Deaf Paul grinned at it.
Deaf Paul supposed that pretending to be dinosaurs was a new
trend. He picked up a pebble and pelted it at the T-Rexasaurus's head. Before it could turn and spot him, Deaf Paul fell
through an uncovered manhole and passed out.

The real T-Rexasaurus stomped on. It wasn't going to go
crashing through ceilings. It was going to slink, eat, and wait.

*

After a brief recess in which Casper laughed and Sixteen pinched
his thighs, President Captain announced that they were beginning again. Sligo stood. He didn't look defeated. Casper tried to
look up his sleeve and toppled over.

'I'd like to call witnesses,' Sligo said.

'Go on.'

First, he called the sculptors, who walked awkwardly to the
front and admitted having seen late night lights at The Cardboard Hill. Casper squinted and claimed insomnia.

Second, he called the seamstress, who had sold Casper
reams of latex and leather. Casper said he had been renovating
his home. Waterproofing the ceiling and strengthening the walls
and so on.

Third, he called the glass blower who reported a crowbarred
door and missing shards. Casper said nothing.

Lastly, he called the mechanic who had seen Casper near
George Stanza's shipping container the night before the hand
broke through the sky. Casper winced and shrugged and refused
to look at Sixteen.

The mayor turned to talk to his council. They spoke for half
a minute. He turned back to the crowd and stood and raised his

arms like antenna. 'The jury find you guilty of making Tatiana P cry and everyone really scared.'

'I find the jury guilty of being massive trousersnakes.'

'We sentence you to go into jail until forever.'

'Fine.'

The mayor expected applause as Casper was forced into a sleeping bag, zipped up to his chin, and carried away. There was no applause. The only celebration was Kevin's whooping, followed by more shouting.

'We want to know about the hand!'

'And the penguins!'

'Nobody cares about the penguins.'

'Is the night coming?'

'We care about the penguins!'

'That's her again doing a different voice.'

'The mayor is making the night come. He's an idiot and he loves the night.'

'If you love the night so much, why don't you marry it?'

'Burn the mayor!'

'Listen,' said the mayor. 'I'm sorry. I'm trying. I don't know what to do. A giant hand came out of the sky. I'm scared too. What are we supposed to do? There's nothing we can do. There's nothing.' He clenched uncertainly, hoping that honesty was enough.

'That's your plan?'

'The plan is do nothing!'

'Great plan, idiot.'

The mayor was shielded by his council and walked away, sobbing and shaking, his wife tailing the party with both hands flat against her head.

*

Diana wasn't at the trial. She was at the house with Halli Galli, methodically identifying her own possessions, carrying them outside, and loading them onto a trailer hitched to a tricycle. Halli Galli was Diana's closest friend. She was four years old and sold piñatas shaped like alligators in Little Montenegro.

'It's best you're leaving,' she said.

'I know,' Diana said.

'It's best you're not with him.'

'I know.'

Diana didn't think it was best. She wanted to be with him but she also wanted Casper Font evicted from his head. She didn't understand why he still spoke for his friend even after it was obvious what he'd done. Halli Galli had wet herself four times since the first announcement concerning the arrival of the dinosaurs. Diana had cried. The baker's nose had leaked blood and the cobbler's knees had surrendered and three of the five clock toss cheerleaders had sleepwalked into carp hatcheries.

Diana would have made an ultimatum before leaving, only she considered ultimatums to be tacky, spiky things, and a refuge for the selfish. She wondered if she was being selfish and decided that she wasn't. She added a singing fish to the trailer.

*

President Captain spoke to no one. He locked himself in his study, drew the curtains, and taped over the keyhole. A pinball machine stood in one corner of the room. It was space themed, with the idea being that each ball, when launched, became an astronaut who had to survive on various planets for as long as possible. This was the safe. President Captain achieved a score of exactly 13221, entered his name as Diego Santana, and stood back as the front of the machine swung open.

Inside was a book that had only ever been read by mayors and kings. It was a secret text that was passed down. Considered too likely to incite fear in Billions, it had never been made public.

He fell into a chair and began reading for the hundredth time.

If anyone finds this, be scared. Please, it will help. They are up there and they are not our friends.

I write this from inside a steel box that has been welded shut around me. I have been tasked with recording our final hours. The sirens howl and the people howl and the river waters eat everything. The night is here. The night came.

My wife's hand is in my pocket, still covered in the whales she drew over her knuckles when she got bored. My wife had her throat torn out by a snow leopard. I tore out that leopard's eyes.

I am Sibelius Maria. I am The Candy King.

All hail The Candy King.

President Captain took a break to do forward rolls on the floor. He wondered how The Candy King had kept his people from revolting. Maybe he hadn't kept his people from revolting. Maybe he had been sealed into the box against his will and maybe the only person to have tasked him with writing the book was himself. President Captain hoped not.

He got up and returned to the book.

First came the dinosaurs. They stalked the streets like scouts, sometimes bowing to attack, mostly building maps for the waves that would come next. We lost people to the dinosaurs, yes. We lost people but it was nothing compared to what would come after.

At least there weren't dinosaurs yet. That was something. Not something huge, but something. And maybe there wouldn't be dinosaurs at all. Maybe the hand really was nothing.

What followed was every nightmare.

Holes.

Ghosts.

Devils.

Things we didn't recognize.

The town was picked up and pulled apart. There is now almost no one left. I don't know what use this will be except to prepare you. You know that the night is coming. The end is coming. They are coming. Do not try to fight.

Men have hurled clocks through the clouds and those men have had their arms torn off and forced down their throats.

All hail the Candy King.

The mayor crawled beneath his desk, pulled his t-shirt up over his face, and fell asleep. He dreamed of lightening storms and tigers with blank faces. He dreamed of electric webs over black water and blue clouds and dismembered limbs riding hurricanes. He thumped the carpet beside him until his knuckles bled.

*

Emilia War's birthday party begun the same way all birthday parties begun: with attendees taking it in turns to deliver blows to her body that corresponded with the number of years she had existed. Emilia War had existed for five years. She was sitting on the counter at the Milk Bar facing a queue of people keen to vent their frustration.

A band consisting of steel drum, viola, and three recorders, played from a stage made of shoeboxes. The Vess twins' XYOYX. Platters of Neapolitan ice cream cake sat on each table. Jugs of milk were being passed along chains of people crammed together.

Tatiana P wasn't at the party. She hated birthdays and hid from them as though they were bears. It was a fear learned from her father, who had sworn and thrown paperweights if ever her voice got soft on an April 6th.

Kevin was at the party. He was waiting for his turn to strike Emilia War, trying to decide where to hit and settling on the clavicle. Somewhere he had never been permitted to handle Tatiana. It's a legitimate phobia, she had said. I don't have to explain myself to you.

A hand knocked on his shoulder. It was Kimya Cole, dressed in an oversized t-shirt and chewing her hair.

'Leave me alone,' he said.

'Mr Grateful.'

'I didn't need help.'

'We both need help.'

Someone in a corner shouted *Niagara*, prompting a wave of Billions pouring drinks over each other's heads. The last one to empty his glass would be made to break it on his face. Kimya Cole emptied hers on Kevin's head. Kevin emptied his in his own lap.

'I don't need help. I'm a lone... thing.'

'There are meetings.'

'A lone wolf.'

'Take this.' He closed his eyes. 'What are you doing? Take it.'

He opened his eyes. She wasn't going to hit him. She was proffering a lilac card. He glanced at it, pocketed it, and turned to take his turn punching the birthday girl.

'Happy birthday,' he said, breaking her clavicle.

Midway through their final song, the Vess twins were lifted into the air and passed over the sea of heads. Ryan panicked and beat the heads with his recorder, shouting at them to set him down. Neil was grinning. He jabbed the air with his fists and improvised sounds.

When arms got tired, the twins were dropped onto stools at the bar and gifted milkshakes.

'What was that?' Ryan said.

Neil dunked his nose into his drink. 'What was what?'

'What they did.'

'They like us. We're the best.'

'Really?'

'I think so.'

Ryan looked over his brother's shoulder. Several Billions raised glasses and cheered. 'They like us,' he said.

'I know.'

A spike of electricity jumped from one of Ryan's ears to the other. 'You know what we should do?'

Neil didn't know what they should do. 'Yeah,' he said. 'Star Wars.'

'No. We should do one of those things... We should get a group of people who hate the mayor and all hate the mayor together and get Casper out of jail and save the town from whatever stupid massive hands are hiding up there.'

'Yeah,' Neil said, laughing at the butcher, who had tripped over his own foot. 'What?'

'The mayor is ruining this town. He's going to kill us all. We can stop it.' He climbed onto his stool and smashed his glass against the ceiling. 'Burn the mayor!' he howled, spit flying from his mouth.

'Burn the mayor!' Halli Galli repeated.

'Burn the mayor!' everyone chanted.

Glasses shattered.

Shoes flew.

Blood vessels burst.

The birthday girl had passed out. Billions didn't notice. They continued to sink fists into her until the swarm of bruises gave the appearance of something that was rotting.

*

Support Group
    For People Who Are
    Extremely Scared
    Of The People
    They Want
    To Stand
    Very Close To:
    Every 4th
    Olive green
    Aquarium
    Basement

*

Avery rode the train towards the tearoom with his head spinning through images of his best friend hanging half dead from meat hooks in underground bunkers. His carriage was empty. He drew concentric circles in the dust on the window glass.

He'd always guessed that laughing at things he didn't understand was a tactic Pele used as a moat. He didn't think that when the moat dried out it would lead to here, now. He didn't think Pele would ever be stupid enough to seek refuge in The Jungle.

Neither of them had been tested.

Always warm and full and surrounded.

There had never been anything so solid to throw rocks through.

He disembarked at the canal and entered the tearoom. Aside from Eliza Seuss, the only other occupant was a small person in a rabbit suit with his nose pressed to the glass.

'Can I get you something?' Eliza Seuss asked.

He ordered peppermint tea and took a seat as close to the window but as far from the rabbit as possible. He stared at the wall of trees across the water, then at his knees. Kelis had told him to expect huge and hungry beasts, unlike anything anyone had ever seen. She'd tried to go with him. She'd insisted. He'd knocked her out with a golf club while she was using the toilet and left after writing a short note.

I'd rather lose myself than you. Try not to start eating butter blocks again. And don't worry. I'll be back in time for the next Tentacle Festival.

'Here,' Eliza Seuss said, setting down a china cup.

'I was wondering if you could help me with something?'

'Possibly.'

'I'm looking for someone. He's kind of chubby and sweats a lot. One of his eyes is blue, the other is green. He might have come through here.'

'I saw him. He rented a boat and went to The Jungle. He hasn't brought it back.'

He really had gone into The Jungle.

Stupid, stupid, stupid.

'I'd like to rent a boat.'

'This way.'

He swallowed his tea in one gulp and scalded his throat. He followed Eliza Seuss below the teahouse, pushed a heap of numbers into her hands, and got into the nearest boat. It was cramped and his knees stood level with his shoulders.

'Be careful,' she said. 'A lot of people have been heading that way recently. None of them come back.'

It was something he'd repeated but never really believed. 'None?'

She shook her head.

'Thanks.'

He pushed off from the side, rowed out from under the tearoom, and set out across the canal.

It didn't take long to cross directly. The water was still and the wind was low. On the other side, he hauled the canoe onto the land and covered it with fallen tree branches. It wasn't well hidden but based on what the waitress had said there would be no one around to try and take it.

His first steps were tentative. When nothing ate him, he sped up. He ran without stopping, past repeating clumps of trees and hovering eyes. He ran for longer than he had ever slept. He ran until something snapped and a net swallowed his body.

Hanging dumbly high above the jungle floor, Avery couldn't lose the feeling that he was about to be eaten. He didn't know what would eat him. He guessed a lion dressed in human clothes.

As the sky changed, The Jungle darkened. Avery Vitafit curled into a ball and wet himself, yellow pee lashing his face.

*

Casper was alone and afraid. His new cell was windowless. The other cells were empty. He'd tried screaming and gotten no response. The jailor was prone to napping for extended periods of time. He was deaf in one ear, afraid of mirrors, and incapable of urinating while standing.

Casper rearranged himself on the bare floor and repeatedly beat himself in the temples. He pictured Tatiana's face when George had revealed himself and sobbed and scratched. He pictured her tiny hands clapping as George was carried through the clouds.

The Dream Nurse wouldn't have clapped.

I am the worst person in the world and I need your help.

He'd done something wrong and he didn't know why.

It didn't make sense. Tatiana P didn't make sense. He was tied to her by something he couldn't see. He was continually tripping over the tether.

And The Dream Nurse had tricked him. She'd told him the dream said he should go ahead and her advice had led to this. He didn't blame her. He blamed himself for chasing a blank doll instead of a person, warm and wet and alive.

Now he'd be forgotten.

He'd grow and shrink and disappear in the cell.

He napped fitfully and tried to rebuild the outside for himself.

He thought of cities under oceans and attics and loud cows. He thought of cardboard boxes filled with clothes and plastic boxes filled with dead light bulbs. He thought of cobwebs and blue cheese. He thought of naps. He thought of blackcurrant jam and hiding under the dinner tables of strangers. He thought of goosebumps beside swimming pools. He thought of too hot baths and too small blankets. He thought of lions. He thought of castles and wooden swords and pieces of string in tiny pockets. He thought of the feeling of preparing to be struck and the feeling of pulling on your own genitals and the feeling of flight. He thought of tricycles and pillows. He thought of the voices above the clouds. He thought of himself stretching up toward them like a plant towards the sun.

Time stretched and the sky changed.

*

Fuchsia
    Magenta
    Cerise
    Raspberry

Terra cotta
    Salmon
    Tangerine
    Rust

Pistachio
    Olive
    Mint
    Teal

Cerulean
    Cornflower
    Egyptian
    Ultramarine

*

The second person to see the real T-Rexasaurus was Halli Galli. It was late. Cerulean light swamped the streets.

She was out buying pastries for her and Diana at The

Anytime Bakery. The two of them had eaten everything else in the house. They'd played snap for hours and pierced each other's ears with safety pins. Neither of them wanted to sleep. They wanted to sit in blanket piles and trade theories about the above in order to keep Dr Sixteen out of Diana's head.

As she crossed the turpentine stream, by way of several triangular stepping stones, it appeared ahead of her.

It was a dark, unidentifiable mass of black until the light caught its teeth as it lumbered forward, enveloping her body in its jaw.

She headbutted the roof of its mouth and stamped its tongue with her heels. She hollered down its throat and thumped its cheeks. The T-Rexasaurus didn't notice. It bit her in half and swallowed her whole. Goodnight, Halli Galli.

A,

I'm at a desk. Watching rain drop past the streetlights. Drinking beer. Pushing my heels against a radiator.

I'm back now.

I'm living with my nan.

On the first night, she bought me a box of beer. We sat together in the living room. I drank. She did a puzzle of three giraffes walking through an African sunset. She enjoys hearing about the royal family. They'd recently done something. Gone somewhere. Made a speech. So we channel hopped for news coverage of that. Everything's calm here. There's not much I can do wrong. There's not enough room to fall over.

I finished the beers before she went to bed. Then I went looking in the drinks cabinet. There was still a bottle of Lamb's in the back filled with apple juice. From when we had the last school disco.

Do you still talk to anyone from school?

I talk to Kevin.

That's it though. He's the only one.

Today I asked if he remembered when we all snuck out of the last disco. He said she didn't. Do you? You told everyone in our class to meet on the roof. You didn't want to be next to anyone we didn't want to be next to. We drank. And smoked. And gave each other dead legs. Chris Pellman tried to give a speech. Everyone shouted 'gay' at him until he stopped talking. Neil threw a bottle. It broke Mr Gunderson's windshield. We hid in the canoes that are kept up there for reasons none of us knew. You didn't have a house key when we got to your house. We slept in your dad's car. That was the last time we had sex. I remember apologizing a lot afterwards. I remember always apologizing.

Except the first time. The first time I ran to the upstairs bathroom. You ran to the downstairs bathroom.

I've been rereading old books that make things feel safe. People say to write what you want to read. I want to rewrite every Murakami book, word for word. It will take a long time. But I think I can do it,

    C

Five.

XYOYX met for the first time to eat breakfast in The Queen's, on account of The Milk Bar being frequented by members of the mayor's council. The barman at The Queen's held open his arms. Aside from extra income, he wanted Casper out as much as they did. He didn't know if Casper was responsible. He didn't care.

The tables in the bar had been arranged into one long table that divided the bar neatly in two. The Vess twins sat at the heads. Other Billions present included the butcher, the remaining clock toss cheerleaders, several sculptors, an ice climber, Kimya Cole, Kelis Vitafit, Fizika, Angelica, and The Boy Who Eats Glass. Ned Kloot had abandoned the pachinko machine to be present. A radio played cicadas.

Ryan Vess hammered the table with his mug, dousing himself with tea. 'Good morning,' he said. 'Thank you for coming to the first meeting of XYOYX, a committee to get rid of the stupid mayor and save Billion.'

People cheered and globs of egg white flew between them.

'Our first order of business is what we should be called and me and Neil think we should be called XYOYX and we invented it so—'

'We should be called The Penguins,' Angelica said. She was breaking a Cumberland sausage into chunks and passing them to a German Shepherd she sometimes liked to pretend was waiting beneath whichever table she ate at.

'No one's afraid of penguins.'

'We should be called Ella Peti.'

Neil Vess climbed beneath the table. He spotted the chunks of sausage and crawled over to them.

'We should be called this.' A clock toss cheerleader completed a hand dance while rapidly blinking and flicking her hair.

'Well,' said Ryan Vess. 'All in favour of XYOYX.' Everyone chewed. 'Passed.'

The barman ducked around the table until all the food had been set out and the teapots were full. He lit several gas lamps, closed the blinds, and took a seat.

'Next, I thought we should agree on what we think and what we should do and whatever.' He paused to fit a wad of bacon into his mouth. 'I wrote this down and I thought I could just read it and if anyone thinks any part is wrong just say.'

He coughed.

'We are XYOYX and we hate the mayor. The mayor put Casper Font in jail and Casper Font is the best and he should come out of jail.'

'Objection,' said a sculptor, slapping Ryan Vess. 'Cassius Benjamin is the best.'

'Overruled,' said Ryan Vess, continuing. 'The mayor is not on our side.

The mayor is a two out of ten.

He wants the night to come and he knows the night is coming and he is doing nothing about it. A hand came and his plan was to do absolutely zero and have us all die.'

There were nods. Ned Kloot tentatively dipped his nose into a bowl of hot chocolate. His skin burned and peeled away.

'If we agree on that, we need to agree on a plan for getting rid of him. He's got the police and probably secret weapons and probably a rhino.'

'We could put food in his shoes,' said Kelis Vitafit. 'Meat patties and hamburgers and so on.'

'We could spread a rumour that he was born of a horse's vagina.'

A sculptor high fived another sculptor.

'Barbed wire,' Ned Kloot said. 'Barbed wire and also chicken wire.'

'Could you expand?'

'I don't think so.'

The Ice Climber stood. His face was square and his neck

was like a mound of roots. 'We should use fire and force,' he said. 'We should launch an attack on City Hall and force the mayor into surrender.'

'Great,' said Ryan Vess. 'You should probably be captain or leader or whatever. Who votes this person as captain?'

'No, you're leader. From now on, you'll be The Admiral. I'll be your advisor. I can help. I've fought before.'

'I'm the Admiral,' said Ryan Vess grinning. 'Where's Neil?' Neil gingerly resurfaced from below the table, his mouth wet with grease. 'Neil, I'm The Admiral. What do you think?'

'Yes, loads.'

'When do we start?'

'We start tonight.'

Neil Vess laughed hysterically, swinging back on his chair and knocking a platter of salami to the floor. 'What, Neil?'

'What Neil?' said Neil. 'This Neil! Nothing.'

'Do you have a plan?' asked The Admiral.

'Yes,' said The Ice Climber. 'We'll need drums, paper planes, candles, city maps, and weapons. We'll need to be loud. We'll need to move fast.'

*

Since Casper's arrest, The Dream Nurse had started sweating so profusely that there was a constant puddle beneath her feet. She'd never read a dream wrong. She knew what it looked like. He'd asked her for her help and now he was trapped in a jail cell alone.

Immediately after the trial, she'd begun chain drinking pints of milkshake and scrutinizing the dreams that followed. She'd mixed flavours, added inanimate objects at random, and vomited fourteen times.

The dreams all said to wait and to listen.

Looking for an explanation, she went up to the roof of her

house, snatched a wren from the sky, and turned it inside out. The streets below were swirling with tides of Billions. A paper plane skidded to a stop at her feet.

*

Do you think the mayor is the worst mayor out of all the mayors ever?

Do you want to tear his ears from his head with your hands?

Do you want to undress him and burn him to the ground? We do too!

Join XYOYX today as we march on City Hall.

President Captain is best friends with the night…

Let's be best friends with each other!

*

Avery was jabbed awake with spears. He screamed and thrashed like a shark in the net. The people below him were laughing and gibbering and spinning their staffs like batons.

'What are you doing?' he shouted. 'Stop doing it.' He gripped the highest rung of the net and raised his body as though doing a pull up.

'Look,' someone said, almost crying. 'Look, look.'

'Trying to hide!'

'Try harder!'

There were fourteen of them. They wore nothing but multiple pairs of underwear and headdresses made of crow feet. Their bodies were covered in dense black hair. Each had a belly that drooped like a basset hound's jowl. Two basset hounds wove between their legs, barking and swatting mosquitos with their tails.

'Let me go, please. I'll give you numbers and a car and my house and you can be even on the radio if you want to be on the radio.'

A thrown knife cut the trap from the tree and Avery fell, his prison opening around him like a flower. He landed on the damp feet of the largest person. One of the dogs tasted his cheek.

The largest person was called J23. Every person's name consisted of a letter followed by a number. It avoided the confusion of same names in a place where the population only grew.

'Wow,' said J23, beaming. 'The radio.' He turned to U887. 'Truss him up.'

'Don't truss me up,' Avery pleaded. He covered his behind with his hands. He didn't know what 'truss up' meant. 'Let me go. I was just looking for my friend. Pele. That's all. I see he's not here. I'll leave.'

'Not until after dinner.'

At this, Avery again began desperately to squirt pee. It ran and dripped and sprayed through his shorts. The people that had been approaching fell backwards, grappling with tree trunks as they bent in half laughing.

'It's pissing itself!'

The collective howl of the tribe shook starlings from the trees. They shot into the sky, assembled into formations, and flew toward The West Wall.

'Please don't eat me,' Avery said. 'I'll do anything.'

'I won't eat you, if you don't eat me.'

'I won't eat you.'

'Do you promise?'

'I promise.'

J23 made an L with his fingers and held it under his chin. 'I don't believe you,' he said. 'You've got one of those faces.'

'No I don't. I really don't. Look.'

As Avery fervently tried to rearrange his features, T4, P77, and U887 bound his hands and feet. T21 snapped a low branch from the nearest tree. They slid it through his bonds, hoisted it onto their shoulders, and carried him through The Jungle. While they walked, they sang. Songs about girls, bubblegum, and daytime naps. J23 blew birdcalls through a bowl made from his hands. Replies whistled in from the distance.

*

Shape brought ciabatta bread, Parma ham, peppermint tea, and mango, to Pele in the third storage hall. Pele hadn't slept. He smiled weakly, gave up attempting handstands, and toppled to the earth floor.

'Not so much sleeping?' Shape asked.

Pele shook his head. 'No handstands either. It's so hard.'

'This is not hard.'

Shape set down the breakfast basket and flapped his hands, indicating that Pele should try again. Pele flashed his wrists in confusion. 'Try,' said Shape.

Pele repositioned his head into what had now become a crater in the ground and kicked upwards. Shape placed one palm on Pele's bellybutton and another on the root of his spine. His student shook but held. Once sure of Pele's stability, Shape joined him.

They both stood vertically upside down.

'You need to be sleeping,' said Shape. 'Your eyes look like you are being always punched.'

'Bad dreams.'

'Today I go into town. I tell you later how are the people.'

'Thank you. Is that food?'

'Yes, this food.'

They ate in candlelight, sitting on upturned coal buckets at a boxcar topped with a pane of stained glass. Shape barely ate. He never ate much. Everything he consumed dripped immediately through him. Instead, he watched Pele's unrelenting hunger with amusement and fascination, as though it were the mating ritual of an exotic reptile.

'This is so good. Where do you get this?'

He produced a circle of card with I O U one mango written on it, and explained that he'd taken a stack of them from The Debt Museum.

The Parma ham had been inside a giant glass bottle that he'd caught while fishing the canal. With it had been a note that read *Oh Mercurio, he stole my heart and unscrewed my feet, send help, please, even pigeons could lift me now.*

The bread was made in the kitchen.

'And I am picking peppermint from Jungle.'

'You go into The Jungle?'

'Skirt The Jungle, don't go in, no. Never in.'

'I was going to go into The Jungle.'

'This is a very terrible, very bad idea.'

'Maybe.'

'Why going in?'

'It's better than town.'

'No.'

'Why? What's in there?'

'Kind of people trap, trapping people, trap, trap.'

'You aren't scared of being trapped?'

'Impossible.'

After they had finished eating, Pele led Shape back to the site of their first meeting. His nest had grown into a queen size bed built of bridal veils, bridesmaid dresses, bow ties, and cummerbunds.

'You've been nice to me,' he said. 'Thank you.' He whipped a tartan blanket off a mound between junk stacks and revealed a rebuilt pyramid of teeth. 'I fixed your weird tooth thing.'

They stared at each other.

Shape crushed the toes of one foot with the heel of the other. He ran to his bedroom, vomited black ink over his bedsheets, and collapsed. The ink made a black dog beneath his chest. He dreamed he woke up in The Burrow and no light switches would work. He was powerless.

Pele front flipped into the pyramid of teeth and opened a hundred cuts in his calves.

*

Diana woke up and realized that she'd fallen asleep. She searched the house for Halli Galli. Halli Galli was not in the bathtub or the washing machine or under the bed or asleep on the highest bookshelf. The last thing she remembered was her friend leaving to get pastries from the bakery. She dressed and left the house, intending to retrace that route.

The town was unusually awake. People stood in huddles, rubbing their hands, putting their fingers in each other's nostrils, and mumbling. Flocks of paper planes cut through the streets. Several pestered Diana, asking to be opened and read. She tore them into confetti and tossed them over her shoulders.

When the light became terra cotta, she reached the turpentine stream and found a birthmark of blood on the cobbles. She crouched, unable to breathe, running her hands over the ground.

Nothing.

Glass crumbs.

Nothing.

Safety pin.

Nothing.

A pink plastic earring in the shape of an alligator.

She went dumb. Her head said that there were no dinosaurs and that there was still a Halli Galli, somewhere in Billion, warm and unharmed, chewing gum and leafing through coffee table books. Her stomach said that it wanted to leap out of her mouth. She tried to ignore her belly and focus on delivering instructions to her limbs.

Go to the mayor.

Tell the mayor.

Ask the mayor.

She caught The Walking Bus into The Circle. Walking buses were chains of Billions holding hands. At either end of the chain were people with metal baseball bats, crossbows, and blowpipes. Walking buses ran during periods of scared and heavy noise.

At City Hall, Diana found the receptionist asleep on a pillow of marine themed colouring books. Her ponytail had been snipped off and it lay beside her like a pet.

There were no obstructions on the staircase or along the corridor. The mayor's office was unlocked. She swung open the door to reveal President Captain, lying prone on his carpet, wearing a Batman suit and reading a book as deep as a mug.

He squawked and lobbed the tome behind his desk.

'Who are you?' he asked. 'Guards!'

She strode toward him, arms raised as though she was being arrested. 'I think there really is a dinosaur.'

'What do you want?' He heaved himself up and refused to meet her eyes.

'To tell you that I think there really is a dinosaur.'

President Captain circled around his visitor, heading for the door. 'There really isn't a dinosaur.'

'My friend went missing. I went out to look for her and instead found a huge blot of blood and her earring and crumbs of glass.'

President Captain pictured his blackened cadaver amid the ruins of City Hall. He pictured his corpse being dismembered and juggled. He pictured his wife's nose being infiltrated so often and by so many fingers that her septum fell into her lap.

'I'm sorry,' he said, taking a brass toad from his bookcase and pitching it at her head.

It struck Diana between the eyes.

She fell.

The mayor closed his door. He bound her hands and

feet with the telephone cable and the lamp cord respectively, opened the bookcase door, and rolled her into his annex.

*

'What are you going to do?' Kevin asked. He was sitting opposite Tatiana P at their kitchen table. She was squeezing a teabag soaked in boiling water with her bare hand. Dribbles ran down her chin.

'I'm going out.'

When he looked at her, Kevin still saw a pristine, exotic planet of rainbow grass and glassy waters. When she said angry things, he saw vicious, marauding blots on the landscape that it was his responsibility to extinguish.

'Oh.'

'Don't oh me.'

'Sorry.' He pulled a tangerine segment out of the globe in his hands and swallowed it. 'Where are you going?'

'I don't have to tell you that. I'm not your pet.'

'I know.'

'You can't lock me up. I don't belong to you.'

Please, Kevin thought. Please can I do that. Please can I lock us both up so deep under the ground that our ceiling is a web of fossils and a lava ball is our closest neighbour.

*

The sky switched through pistachio, olive, and mint, as teams of XYOYX followed the paths through the town designated to them by The Ice Climber. They bleated into tinhorns, pasted posters over billboards, launched paper planes, and chanted. The teams swelled with each lap. Billions emerged from their homes beating colanders with wooden spoons and tearing apart papier mâché models of the mayor. Others stood on their balconies and rooftops, afraid. Those people had voted for the mayor and liked him and saw nothing tying him to the hand or the oncoming night. Some upturned toilet bowls on the parades that passed under them. Some got into bed. Some went to the mayor with warnings and promises of allegiance, asking for reassurances and bowls of comfort food.

*

Deaf Paul regained consciousness. He was not surprised to find himself somewhere unfamiliar. It happened often when he binge drank milk and forgot to sleep.

He couldn't remember binge drinking milk.

He sat up.

He could remember walking the rice pudding terraces. Empty streets. Coming home. Whistling. Feeling hungry. Picturing helicopters hovering over volcanoes.

He could remember a dinosaur that bucked when he hit it with a stone.

A real dinosaur?

He hoisted himself up and out of the sewer, located The Globe in the distance, and began to sprint toward The Circle. As he ran, he tripped and fell and tripped and fell. His knees were red mobiles of skin at City Hall.

The mayor was pacing when Deaf Paul entered his office. His head was sweaty and crammed with the woman in his annex and the dinosaurs and the hand.

'DINOSAUR,' Deaf Paul said.

'Get out.'

'DINOSAUR.'

'Go.'

'HELP.'

President Captain ripped a square of paper from his post-it stack, scrawled on it, and stuck it to his own forehead.

You are no longer on the council.
Leave my office.
Never come back.

'Dinosaur,' Deaf Paul whispered, blinking out tears and making a rapid exit out into the swarming city.

*

Dr Sixteen's response to Diana's evacuation of their home was to make his way through the jostling crowds towards Halli Galli's house in Little Montenegro. He knew that was the only place she'd be. He knew a lot of things about her. He knew she liked her left foot more than her right, clouds more than a clear sky, tea over sleep. He knew she refused to use hairdryers in empty houses and that she was afraid of turtles and had dreams in which they pecked at her favourite toes with their beaks until all that was left were rods of bone protruding from bloody stumps. He knew she mistrusted milk. He knew she'd leave and that he'd go after her.

No one answered Halli Galli's door. Sixteen broke in through a window and flipped everything that could be flipped upside down until he was sure she wasn't there.

He went back out into the crowds and fought through swarms of shoulders, asking everyone where his wife could be, and getting nothing in response except paper planes and invitations to City Hall.

'I need to find my wife,' he shouted. 'I'm scared.'

'The mayor probably did it,' someone told him. 'He's the worst. Come with us.'

'Yes.' Someone else fitted a block of sushi into his hand. 'Come with us.'

'Leave me alone.'

Dr Sixteen chased through Billions, indiscriminately batting them with open palms and eliciting indignant cries in response. He ran at random, through suburbs he'd never seen, over bridges he didn't know existed, and past people he didn't want to exist. His wife was prone to overreactions but even when feeling dramatic she never left either their home or her best friend's. She never left.

*

Avery swung like a pendulum hanging from the branch he was lashed to. They walked for a long time. Birds and reptiles parted in waves around them. The L tossed pinecones at each other's heads. They kicked and tripped, pulled faces, thumbed each other in the ears.

The Jungle darkened.

It slowed down.

Sounds grew deep into rumbles.

The film that played in Avery's head was of his wife going after him when he failed to return. Of her being eaten too. The L skewering her nipples with cocktail sticks and roasting them over cave fire. Cutting away her nose and stewing it with basil. Gnawing her still flinching fingertips.

He should have told her that when he had the chance.

I don't want anyone to eat your nipples.

Except me, and only when you die.

Eventually, the settlement came into view. Avery briefly forgot that he was on the verge of being eaten. It was huge. It was high in the trees. Hundreds of turreted wooden huts hugged the trees like koalas. Each was linked by a rope bridge, most of which were missing several slats and lacked handrails. The houses were arranged in a web, with a circular wooden platform hanging in the very centre, blue fires burning in mason jars around its edges. 'Let's start the fire.'

*

Under a cornflower ceiling of sky, the whole of Billion became hysterical as XYOYX marched through the streets, rallying and chanting and elbowing each other in the eyeholes. When the group reached City Hall, it consisted of almost half the citizens of Billion.

Elgar had seen them swell and so had summoned the police to form a blockade in front of City Hall. The policemen wore plastic centurion helmets topped with red mohawks. They held wooden shields painted with dragons and wooden swords with rope handles. DI Dolo stood behind them, on a stack of upturned milk crates, determined not to be the first of his family to let a mayor be torn apart.

'Stop,' he said, into a megaphone fixed to a harmonica bracket. 'Or we'll stab you until you're dead.'

'We'll stab you back!'

'And more times!'

'And in the hole!'

The Ice Climber lifted The Admiral onto his shoulders. 'We want to talk to the mayor,' he said, into a rolled up piece of card he'd presumed would work like a megaphone. It didn't. His voice fluttered and fell like a balloon losing air.

'What did you say?'

He consulted with The Ice Climber, who decided that the only way to make themselves heard was to speak in unison. The message was relayed from hand to ear until it sat waiting in everyone's head. Ryan Vess did a three finger countdown and XYOYX spoke at once.

'We want to speak to the mayor,' they said, half singing.

'The mayor doesn't want to speak to you,' DI Dolo said. 'The mayor wants you to go away.'

President Captain opened the doors to his balcony and

tentatively stepped out, Lucille behind him, clutching the fabric of his shirt. He spoke into the microphone mounted on his cherub statue.

'Oh my god,' he said, taking them in. Rows of drooling citizens clasping unlit Molotov cocktails, all lit from below by candles inside mason jars. They revved their feet against the tarmac.

'I know, right?' said Neil Vess, speaking into his brother's ersatz megaphone.

'What are you all doing down there?' President Captain watched The Admiral's mouth move and caught nothing. He gestured for the police to hand over their megaphones. 'What are you doing?' he said again.

'We're going to set you on fire because you're stupid and we hate you.'

The mayor turned his wife. They conferred with their eyes and reached the conclusion that they were in trouble. 'No,' he told them. 'Don't do that. That's a terrible idea.'

Neil Vess whispered to Ryan Vess. 'Okay,' he said. 'We're still going to do it.'

Someone threw a mason jar. It split President Captain's forehead and ricocheted back into the crowd. 'Stop that. I'm your mayor. I'm like a king but you chose me.'

'We know what a mayor is.'

'Go back inside to your golden bath and your golden goose.'

'What are you talking about golden goose? All I have is a pinball machine.'

'Nice try, President Suckhole.'

At this, the wall of police lunged forward.

The mayor retreated back into City Hall under a hail of glass and fire, mouthing President Suckhole to himself and chewing lumps off his cheeks. Lucille followed him beneath the desk. She pulled his bent legs to her chest and balanced her cheek on his knees. His eyes were closed.

'We should get into The Bunker.'

The Bunker had been built during the time of Mayor Bunga, in response to predictions of an alien invasion. The plan had been for everyone to dig homes beneath their homes, and to wait in them until the aliens got bored and went away. Aliens never came. Dinosaurs turned up instead.

'No,' he said. 'Shut up.'

'I'm sorry.'

'Don't be sorry, I'm sorry.'

'Well, I'm sorry too.'

'I have to tell you something.'

'Another iguana?'

'I tied up a woman and hid her in the annex.'

'So that you could. . .'

'No, not that. She was going to tell them that a dinosaur is here. Really this time.'

'Is it true?'

'I think so.'

'Does it matter anymore?'

'I don't know.'

'Let's get into the bunker.

'I'm staying overground. I know how this ends if we don't fight. The Candy King way.' He stood and cracked his head on the underside of the desk. A trickle of blood ran down the bridge of his nose. 'I will fight for my people even if they turn on me! Even if they call me President Suckhole and throw things! I will pull the rug from underneath the night and drown it in the dry stream!'

Windows crashed and fell around them, letting in strangled cries and bleats. City Hall shook. Elgar's feet appeared. 'Get up,' he said. 'We need to get into The Bunker.'

President Captain felt his eyes grow hot. 'Okay,' he said. 'Fine.'

*

The Dream Nurse felt like Alice again when she saw it. She hadn't moved from the roof. She'd watched the canals of the town fill with people, then empty in a narrow chain headed for City Hall. She hadn't considered following.

Alice held nothing against the mayor. He was too small to conduct any of this. His name was never spelled out in her dreams. He trembled when he held chopsticks. His forearms were solidly hairless.

This was something greater, something all consuming, falling through the roof of everything.

She knew as soon as the real T-Rexasaurus passed under her awning, that it was destined for the congregation of people facing off with the mayor.

*

Deaf Paul filled a rucksack with all of the milk in his house and set out on an aimless expedition out of The Circle, towards the blank distance. He drank as he walked. His giant legs formed knots and attempted to abandon him. He pictured himself being squeezed out of the city like an ice cube. He'd lose his house, his possessions, the ability to speak, the option of interacting with others. When the night came, he'd be alone. He'd be asleep naked on the floor of nowhere, puddles of milk in the dips of his chest and clotted gum in his hair.

*

Casper was counting ceiling tiles when she opened his cell door. Alice had rendered the guard unconscious by way of a tuning fork to the head. She was sweating. A heavy sickness sat in her stomach.

He doubted she was there. He thought she was another hallucination. Already he'd seen a monkey made of red ants and a fighter pilot with waffles for hands. He'd vanquished them with long, hard breaths and firmly closed eyes.

'You have to come,' she said. He backed into the corner of his cell and buried his face in a cave made of his legs. 'What are you doing? Get up.'

'You're not really there.' She rapped his shin with the tuning fork. 'Fine, you're really there.'

'Thank you.'

He didn't know why she was really there. He guessed she'd come to gloat, to tell him he deserved his new home, and that he'd melt in it like cardboard under heavy rain. It was okay. It wasn't so bad. He had games at least. The guard had learned to pronounce his name. 'You lied to me,' he said.

'You think I'd do that?'

'I wouldn't blame you.'

'Well, I didn't. The dream said to go ahead with your plan. The fake dinosaur is what drew the real dinosaur here. Maybe you needed to fail first to get to now. I don't know. But now you can save the town.'

'There's a real dinosaur?'

'Mm.'

He realized why she'd come and a flash of energy lit him up. He was the dinosaur hunter. If there was a dinosaur, he had something to do. He knew how to do it.

'Aren't you angry? That I set up the first one.'

'It doesn't matter what I am. You're the only one who can help.' Truthfully, she wasn't angry. She was confused, afraid, and a little hungry.

'Why haven't I been let out?'

'They don't know it's there yet. Some people wanted you released, those twins, so they formed a group and now the group has gathered at City Hall.'

'And the T-Rexasaurus is going there?'

'Yes.'

'If it's real, people are going to die.'

'I know. I dreamed it.'

'Let's go.'

A stable of police tricycles were waiting outside of the jail. Casper hitched a trailer to his and a sidecar to Alice's. He told her to collect Cassius Benjamin and bring him to City Hall. He was going to Ned Kloot's. She wrapped one hand around his head and lightly tugged a handful of his hair. They pedaled in opposite directions, the sky above them swimming into a deep Egyptian blue.

*

'You're listening to Nine FM with me, Keira Mary-Kate, standing in for Avery and Pele, who are selfish trousersnakes and have opted not to turn up for work anymore, for reasons that have yet to be ascertained. The sky is currently Egyptian and the cloud count is, according to Milo, somewhere between six and nineteen. I'm sure that will prove desperately useful to you all.

Our top story today: A band of rebel citizens, operating under the name XYOYX, are marching on City Hall in protest of what they see as the mayor's insufficient response to the recent hand through the sky debacle. It is unclear at present what their demands are. More on that in a moment.

Before we move on, I've been asked to bring up the inordinate number of people knocking other people out. While I'm sure some of you have your reasons, most of you really don't, so please stop. Once again, that's no more making each other unconscious. Also, objections are to remain purely verbal. Thank you.

Now to Milo, who's live outside City Hall where, as I understand it, the mayor's police are engaged in a violent engagement with the protestors. Milo?'

'Can I come back to The Globe? I don't think I can do this. It's scary.'

'Where, as I understand it, the mayor's police are engaged in a violent engagement with the protestors. MILO?'

'It hurts. I'm not doing it.'

'What's wrong with you?'

'What's wrong with me is that my head is bleeding. Blood is pouring out of a wide open gap in my head, Keira.'

'Put your hand on it.'

'I am putting my hand on it.'

'Put your hand on it harder, and explain to us all what's happening.'

'What's happening is exactly what you said was happening. They're fighting each other. I don't understand why I always have to go to the places when you know what's happening in them already.'

'Do you want to keep your job?'

'Fine. Here. What's happening is that the people are throwing bomb things and the police are stabbing them and stuff and oh my god.'

'What is it?'

'Oh my god.'

'What?'

'There's a T-Rexasaurus.'

'Another one?'

'A real one.'

'What?'

'There's a dinosaur there's a dinosaur there's a dinosaur.'

'What is it doing?'

'It's eating people and crushing their heads.'

'Describe it.'

'Massive and scary and really really close.'

*

Casper reconvened with The Dream Nurse at the edge of City Hall. His trailer was filled with pachinko balls and the clock he kept hidden under a tarpaulin. Her sidecar was filled with Cassius Benjamin. All three of them shook like wet dogs under the deepening green sky.

'Why did you bring me here?' said Cassius Benjamin. 'You told me I was going to get an award. There are no awards. There's a dinosaur. I'm leaving.'

The T-Rexasaurus was at a reasonably safe distance, snatching Billions from the ground and forcing them into his mouth. The floor beneath it was slick with blood and pools of squashed muscle.

'Um,' Casper said.

'Shut up,' Alice said. 'If you don't do whatever he tells you, it will eat you too.'

'I can't do anything. It's a dinosaur.'

'Shut up,' she said, slapping him. 'Shut up, shut up.'

'You can do something,' Casper said. 'I promise.'

'What do I have to do?'

They huddled and Casper told them his plan. They asked if there was another plan. He said it was the only plan. He said there was a twenty per cent chance of it working and an eighty chance of one of them dying. 'Shotgun not me,' said Cassius Benjamin.

Ryan Vess shot past them. He turned around and shot back. Red handprints marked his face.

'Casper?'

'Ryan?'

'You're out?'

'Alice broke me out.'

'You're going to kill it?'

'I'm going to try.'

'Thank you,' he said, disappearing into the town, to top and tail with his brother under several duvets until the loudness had passed.

Alice, Casper, Cassius, and the trailer of pachinko balls made their way toward the dinosaur. Billions streamed away around them. Others rolled useless on the pavement, groping their stumps, listing in and out of conscious. Cassius used pachinko balls to knock them out. Casper shielded his eyes. The crackle of tearing sinew inside the T-Rexasaurus' mouth grew louder.

They stopped when their hair began to drip saliva. Cassius unloaded the clock from the trailer. Casper nodded.

*

'No,' Avery screamed. 'Please.' The pot below him was filled dark water alive with bubbles. He fought his bonds. His wrists and ankles were burned and bleeding. 'Don't eat me. Do something else. Eat him.'

The L held straight faces. They made grinding motions with their hands and hopped. J23 signaled for the ties to be chopped. The ties were chopped and Avery splashed into the pot. He lunged up and out and hands pressed his face back into the water.

His eyes stung.

His skin didn't shift.

Avery was confused. He wasn't cooking. The L were laughing. They were slapping their bellies and each other and each other's bellies. Two of them helped him out of the pot and set him on the floor of the high wooden platform.

'You didn't cook me.'

'It's bubble bath.'

'You aren't going to eat me.'

'You look like piss.'

They didn't look aggressive anymore. They looked tired and happy. They lay on their backs and uncorked green glass bottles with their teeth. J23 took a seat beside him. 'Don't look so worried, we were joking.'

'Oh,' Avery said. 'Good one.'

'We do it to new arrivals. We find it extremely funny.' He passed his bottle to Avery. Avery sipped from it, held the liquid in his mouth, and dribbled the liquid into his sleeve. 'So funny.'

'I'm not arriving.'

'You've arrived.'

'I mean I'm looking for my friend. Then leaving again.'

'Okay.'

'You really need to leave. All of you. The night is coming. And dinosaurs.'

J23 grinned. He hadn't heard anyone talk about the night since his mouth was too small to hold a whole pinecone. 'Maybe your night is.' He looked at The L, playing catch with their bottles and carving toothy faces into the backs of their hands with glass shards. 'We've been here a long time.'

*

Cassius Benjamin circled the T-Rexasaurus, Casper's clock clamped to his chest. Casper watched a leg disappear between two of the T-Rexasaurus' teeth. He tapped Alice on the elbow. The two of them upturned the trailer, setting a tide of pachinko balls rolling.

At first, the dinosaur balanced awkwardly on its newly uneven sea, unsure of what was happening.

Then it crashed, metal globes embedded in its back, arms thrashing like sharks on hot sand.

'Now,' shouted Casper.

Cassius Benjamin bent his legs, straightened his back, and

launched the clock upward. It peaked over the body of a cheer-leader, its coffin-shaped shadow knocking reflections from her eyes. The dinosaur grunted. The clock landed on its tongue.

It began to fight everything it couldn't see. It wormed so violently that the balls beneath it punctured its skin and were enveloped by muscle. Casper clambered up its sides. His feet found ledges between the scales. He surmounted its face, crawled over its left eyeball, and danced awkwardly on the rim of the dinosaur's nostril.

Undressing, he kept his eyes locked on Alice, who stood beside the best clock tosser in Billion as he ate his fingernails. He tamped all of his clothes into one of the dinosaur's nostrils.

The dinosaur bucked.

Alice shouted. He stumbled and slipped down the hole into a cocoon of phlegm and blood. I'm dead, he thought. And heaven is gross.

Alice ordered Cassius Benjamin to form a stirrup with his hands. He did. She was flung into the air and dove directly into the nostril in which her childhood friend was trapped. The soles of her feet tickled his eyelashes.

'Hi,' she said.

'Heaven is wet,' Casper said.

She twisted and turned and jabbed her fur-covered elbows into the damp walls. It spasmed. It sneezed. The two of them rocketed out, landing in a pile on the dismembered leg of a bubblegum tester. Cassius Benjamin picked them up.

Safe on the ground, the three of them cheered like rescued explorers. The dinosaur was motionless. They haymakered its scales. Nothing. They threw their heels at its skin. It didn't move.

'Is it dead?'

'It looks dead.'

She slid a finger into his nostril and recommenced cheering, pumping her arms and stamping her feet. Everything goes somewhere else now, she thought. 'Stop,' Casper said.

'What?'

He leaped onto the hand that took her. She was too shocked to scream. He bit chunks from the cuticles. 'Let go.'

'No.'

'Put her down.'

'You have to learn to be quiet.'

'Put her down now or else.'

Another hand appeared to brush him off. Cassius Benjamin pinned him by the shoulders as Alice was swallowed by banks of cloud. I don't know what to do, he thought. I'll go to the end. Maybe she'll be there.

*

Billions:

There really was a dinosaur this time.

Really.

Do not leave your houses alone.

Do not leave your houses without things to throw or to hit with.

Do not leave your houses without thought following arguments and tantrums concerning the night and all associated scary seeming things.

Do not refer to scary seeming things as such. Refer to them as 'hilarious jokes' or not at all.

Banana and strawberry milkshakes are now illegal.

Refer to The Dinosaur Manual for more information.

And be calm.

A,

I've been here two months now. I have a routine.

Wake up in the late afternoon. Have tea, smoke, read. Walk the dog around the rugby pitch opposite the house. Watch TV on the TV with Nan. Eat. Try to write. Watch TV on the internet with me. Drink until sleep is easy.

The dog part is probably the best part.

The dog's going to die soon. She has a lot of tumours. Sometimes people reach to stroke her then stop. Every walk is slower than the last. I usually have to take two steps then wait for her to catch up. In one corner of the field she always disappears into one bush for a long time. I hope she's leading a double life. And that the other half happens inside that bush. I hope she's revered and loved and very much alive inside that bush.

I'd like this to carry on. Walking the dog. Watching programmes about antiques. But I think there needs to be another half too. I'm getting restless. I don't want to upset anyone.

Last week I took fifteen sleeping pills. And woke Nan up at 4am to say a girl had disappeared from the hallway. I said the girl was someone I used to know. Nan said we had to go find the girl. We drove laps out in the rain. The girl wasn't anywhere.

The last thing I remember was telling Paul Highton that it was nice to see him. He was sitting on my pillow. I knew he wasn't there.

I was being honest though.

It would be nice to see Paul. I remember when he fell from that tree behind the bike shed. And lost half a finger. And then left school because his parents thought he was being bullied. They thought a bully had ripped off his finger. I don't think anyone would have done that to Paul. People liked him. He was just difficult to talk to.

Do you have a routine? Do you have a job? Are you studying an advanced degree in something somewhere distant? Is it stupid for me to keep asking things? Is it dumb for me to keep talking?

I'm on the sofa. The dog's head is on my crotch. A Miyazaki film is on TV. This isn't so bad. I should probably leave soon,

C

Six.

When Pele woke up he could no longer remember whether his best friend's bellybutton stuck out or sunk in. He guessed out. He couldn't picture it.

He felt more distant even that places he'd never visited.

He had Shape.

Shape was good but Shape was a small, square blanket while he was a naked body shivering on the floor. Shape was there. Shape was coming down the tunnel for breakfast, deliberately clanking cups to alert his visitor and give him getting dressed time. Pele scrabbled the floor for a t-shirt, ran to the nearest wall, and arranged himself in a pile at the bottom of it.

Shape entered. Shape set the table. Shape spotted Pele, looking distressed and unconvincing, his legs hanging over his head at unnatural angles.

'What you are doing?'

'Handstands again. I forgot how.'

'You forget how *how?*'

'I don't know. While I was sleeping, I forgot.'

Again, Shape went to Pele, helped him lift his own weight, and gently sandwiched his stomach between his palms. Pele forced a wobble. Shape pressed harder. And it helped a little, somehow, as though Shape's hands were pushing him closer to something he wanted to be close to. 'Now,' Shape said, dropping his arms. 'We are eating.'

They took seats at the table. The fresh bread steamed. They halved rolls, pasted them with butter, and added translucent slices of ham. Shape poured tea. 'You should be going outside. Do something. Go row.'

'Maybe.'

'Dinosaurs they are not swimming. You know this?'

'I know. What will you do?'

'I go to house I visit always. The man there is never moving. Even if I am very close and breathing like horse. Even if I

127

am playing elephant on the stairs.'

'He has things you want?'

'He has many things. Many boxes with velvet inside and also gold. Earrings and rings and these things. Things without point.'

'Aren't they gifts for his wife or something?'

'No wife. You need me to get anything?'

'Nothing.'

'Good.'

They ate until there was nothing left to eat and carried their plates through to the kitchen. Pele washed and Shape dried. They whistled radio jingles in harmony while they worked.

*

Casper was inside a sleeping bag in the mayor's bunker. He couldn't remember getting into a sleeping bag or the mayor's bunker. Also in the mayor's bunker were: President Captain, Lucille Captain, every member of the council excluding Deaf Paul, the butcher, and Diana.

Casper extricated his arms from the bag and dragged his body over the concrete floor to Diana. A rectangle of silver tape blocked her mouth. He peeled it away and she woke up, afraid at first, then relieved.

'Casper,' she said. 'Thank you.'

'What happened?'

'I don't know. I was telling the mayor about the dinosaur and then I think he knocked me out. Does my head look a different shape? Also, I'm tied up. Can you untie me?' He unzipped her sleeping bag and chewed the rope until it split. Diana wriggled free and sat up. 'What happened?'

'Um.' He swallowed. 'There was a demonstration outside City Hall and then the real T-Rexasaurus came and ate lots of people.'

'Have you seen Sixteen?'

'No.'

'I'm too weak to walk. Will you take me home?'

'Yes, but wait.'

Casper went to the mayor and shook him until he dreamily swatted the air with one hand, shouted 'objection', and opened his eyes. He grinned. 'Dinosaur hunter,' he said.

'Not really,' Casper said. 'I have to go.'

'You can't go. You need to help me.'

'No.'

'Yes.'

'You made Diana unconscious and tied her up.'

'Let's be friends.'

Diana got to her feet and collapsed. She pushed her forehead into the floor and brayed. 'I'll come back later,' Casper said. 'And we can talk. I'm busy now.'

'Great.'

'Great.'

Together, Diana and Casper left the bunker and navigated the corridors of City Hall until they reached its main door. Before they went through, Casper convinced Diana to tie his t-shirt over her face. He led her by the hand around blood puddles and broken bodies and the corpse of the T-Rexasaurus. He removed her blindfold when they turned a corner. They caught a train a train to Sixteen's house in Little Poland.

The door was open. Diana went first, shouting and whistling, turning on every light switch in every room. She stopped in the bathroom. Sixteen was in the bathroom. He was dead in the bathtub.

*

'Casper's the richest person in Billion,' Tatiana said. 'He's got a house and he can ride any albatross any time.'

'Weather permitting,' Kevin whispered. He was eating a

stale bread roll, trying to soften it by dipping it into hot chocolate. Tatiana took them both away. She tapped the roll against her temple and threw it over her shoulder.

'And the girl he likes got eaten.'

'She didn't get eaten. She just went away.'

'How do you know she didn't get eaten? You don't know anything. You can't even tell a dinosaur from a baby in a suit.'

He wanted to crawl under the table but he knew she'd hit him. He wanted to crawl between her legs and curl into a ball. 'You didn't know either.'

'What?'

'Nothing.'

'Here.' She set the mug down under his chin. 'Drink it.'

'Okay.'

Before his lips reached the rim, she gripped his hair in her hands and thrust his face into the mug. It split and tore Kevin's face. He was asleep. She went through his pockets and found four paperclips, two dog biscuits, and the smallest member of a Russian doll team. She took them all to The Kissing Hall, to spend on milk, custard creams, and hand massages.

When Kevin woke up, he dug around in his clothes and found the card given to him by Kimya Cole.

*

Avery sat beside J23 with their legs dangling through the slats of a wooden bridge suspended between trees. Their laps were spotted with beams of light that had broken through the canopy. They held bowls of tea.

'How did you get here?' Avery said. He looked at his feet next to J23's feet and wondered if they were average size for his age.

'The same as everyone. When the night started to come, when holes appeared and people disappeared, I left. I caught a train to the tearoom and rowed across the canal. I walked through the wood for days, until I found here.'

'And they let anyone join?'

'Of course.'

'But there are nets?'

'Because we find it funny.'

Avery tried to imagine leaving Pele and his wife and their house and The Globe. He couldn't. It felt like physical violence. 'You left the town.'

'It wasn't the town anymore. It was something else. And I was afraid of the night. We didn't know what it was. I wanted to sit around drinking milk and throwing clocks and dancing the tentacle dance. I knew the night wouldn't reach the jungle. Nothing reaches the jungle. The jungle is just us. All other rumours are false.'

'All of them?'

'Apart from us.'

'You're really hairy.'

'Thank you.'

'Why?'

'It just happens here.'

'I should really leave.'

'You're staying another day. It's not safe to leave on… todays.' J23 was lying. He didn't know why he was lying. It just seemed somehow important for Avery to wait a little longer.

*

It didn't feel much like anyone had died. How did it feel when someone died? It didn't feel like much. Sixteen, Alice. Casper knew what he was supposed to do. He put Diana into a bed, made himself promise not to climb in next to her, and left the house.

The sky was pale cerise. Nobody was anywhere. The trains weren't running. No birds haunted the clouds.

Casper didn't feel brave. He felt mechanical. His two favourite people were gone. Now he could either do nothing or he could try to stop everyone else losing their favourite people too. He could be The Dinosaur Hunter. For real this time.

The only security at City Hall was two bored policemen milling around the steps doing spit takes with black tea. They thanked Casper and waved him in. At the mayor's office, Casper presented himself to President Captain.

'Thank you for coming,' he said. He swiveled in his swivel chair and stood. 'I knew you would.'

'Um,' Casper said. 'I'm not doing it for you. I don't like you that much. You shouldn't have tied up Diana.'

'Let's be friends.'

'Stop saying that. We can work together. We don't have to be friends.'

'Everyone loves you.' The mayor picked up a paperweight shaped like a hotdog and threw it from one hand to the other. 'They saw you kill the dinosaur. You're the only thing stopping them from drowning themselves. You're the only hope.'

'Um.'

'I've got something you should read before we start. A book. It might help.'

Casper followed President Captain into the annex and accepted The Last Words of The Candy King. He rapidly leafed through it. He stopped on page twenty four.

*

Beware The Tiny Seen, for it will walk amongst you and work in shadows to draw down the curtain of the night. You will not recognize it until all is black. It will stand on pyramids of your bodies and howl into the sky. Beware The Tiny Seen, for it will eat you from underneath. They have gifted it disguise and the pull of a magnet. It will be porcelain or glass, something incapable of being held, something that drifts through the drainpipes and puts into motion a sequence of events that will wake them The Unseen from their slumber. Be careful. And All Hail The Candy King.

*

A banner was hung over the entrance to the aquarium's basement. *Support Group For People Who Are Extremely Scared Of The People They Want To Stand Very Close To.* It was painted in yellow on a stained bed sheet. The door below it was windowless and made of dented metal. Crude drawings of sheep were drawn on in purple marker. Kevin traced one, thinking it to be a cloud. He placed his hand on the handle. He slapped it with his other hand. He placed his other hand on the handle and went inside.

A single light bulb lit a staircase down into the cement room. Billions were sitting on plastic chairs vaguely positioned in a circle. Kevin recognized some of them. The Ice Climber, DI Dolo, Milo from the radio. Kimya Cole wasn't there. If she didn't attend, Kevin didn't know what her connection to the group could be.

'Are we ready?' said Henning Yi. Henning Yi had started SGFPWAESOTPTWTSVCT when he'd been clubbed unconscious and left for dead by someone he'd been standing very close to. A rule of the group was to use false names when referring to people not in the group. Henning Yi referred to his assailant as Mushy Soup. 'It's really sad to see some new faces,' he said. 'Really.'

Kevin covered his face with both hands. He decided that there was no way anyone in the group could help him with anything and he wished he was somewhere else.

'Has everyone been practicing their exercises?' No one answered. 'I have. I only thought about Mushy Soup once this week. It was in the shower. When it happened, I cut off a toe.' He removed one shoe to reveal one remaining toe and a row of exposed bone stumps. Kevin tensed and tried not to cry and wondered if he was going to pass out. 'Who wants to go next?'

DI Dolo stood. 'I thought about Svetlana twice,' he said, lifting up his shirt and exposing two raw circles where nipples had been. 'I thought about her in a cocktail dress and I thought about her in a basket floating on the canal. I threw toenail clippings at my wife. It's just so hard.' A hand reached up and curled over his shoulder. Kevin's cheeks filled with vomit. He swallowed it.

A person Kevin didn't recognize started talking. He didn't stand. 'I thought about Atapee smearing mud into my thighs so I put a ruler into my hole and left it there. I'd show you, but my wife says I'm not allowed.'

'Thank you, Comet.'

'I'd like to go,' The Ice Climber said. 'I'm new. The last time I was with Tatiana was—'

Henning Yi slapped him in the jaw. 'We don't use real names. We use fake names. It's the rules.'

Kevin had already left. He'd skinned his knees on the stairs and was staggering through the streets towards his house. He knew what the club was. It was a club for people Tatiana saw and touched and kissed. Full of people who weren't him. People who'd been allowed into her corners when he hadn't.

She was sitting on the toilet when he arrived. He pushed his thumbs into her throat and pulled it open. She wheezed and then she died. Goodnight, Tatiana P.

Which was when Casper arrived, out of breath and pinching a nosebleed dry. Kevin looked at Casper. Casper nodded. 'I know,' he said. And Kevin seized Casper around the waist, pushing his face into Casper's chest and gently thumping his back.

*

'Hello, Billion. You're listening to Nine FM with me, Keira Mary-Kate. I haven't had a break in seven million sky cycles, Avery and Pele are still missing, and apparently if I leave The Globe then

I'm leaving my job as well. The cloud count is whatever and the sky is whatever and we are all whatever.

Our top story today is that the population of our town is now around half what it used to be, following a violent dinosaur attack during a demonstration at City Hall. The group known as XYOYX had been protesting what they thought to be the mayor's feeble response to a previous incident involving a hand and the sky. They were clashing with police when a T-Rexasaurus appeared from nowhere and began savagely eating, crushing, and maiming those present. The dinosaur was eventually killed by former disgraced Dinosaur Hunter, Casper Font. It is understood that Font is now in talks with the mayor regarding emergency plans and the future of Billion. With us to comment is chief of police, DI Dolo. Hello DI.'

'Hi Keira.'

'The first thing I think everyone wants to know is, why didn't the mayor do anything to prevent this tragedy from happening?'

'Keira, the mayor didn't know this tragedy was going to happen. He thought the hand was just a hand. I mean, most of the time they are. It was an easy mistake to make.'

'If he didn't know, why was he in his bunker with his councilors?'

'He was escaping from the threat of the protestors. It was all getting very violent.'

'And what is the mayor doing to prevent incidents like this happening in the future?'

'As I think you know, Keira, the mayor is in talks with Casper Font, the citizen who actually killed the dinosaur. I'm confident that together the two of them will be able to engineer a plan that will keep everyone left in this town safe.'

'Does the presence of the dinosaur mean that the night is here? Can we expect more events of this nature to unfold?'

'The official line is that yes, Keira, the night is here. And we're doing everything we can to keep it at bay.'

'DI Dolo, thank you very much for talking to us. In other news, just because you say someone's name a lot, doesn't mean they'll like you. Again, that was DI Dolo, the chief of police.

Now, in other other news, reports of strange occurrences have been coming in from across the town. Clay, in Little Poland, says that when she woke up, she found her husbands face floating in their kitchen sink. Paula, in The Coin Mine, says that she woke up with her arms attached to her thighs, forcing her to crawl like a spider up the stairs. And Bethany on Bowl Street says that an identical replica of herself has been chewing her furniture and defecating on her carpet. Terrible stuff there from Bethany. We'll be reading more of your stories as they come in. It is unclear yet whether this really means the night is here. Some have claimed the sky is dimming, while others maintain that some are being idiots. Now for some marine burps to get you off to sleep.'

*

The majority of the remaining Billions had barricaded themselves inside of their homes. They made blanket forts and huddled in them, listening to the radio and drinking milk. No one drank milkshake. They didn't want to know what was or would happen. They wanted it all to go away.

Several citizens had started up businesses selling food, milk, and tea door to door. It was from one of these sellers that Kimya Cole learned about the death of Tatiana P. She clapped when she heard. She dumped a kiss onto the person's forehead and tipped him everything in her fists.

She went to her brother and crouched and whispered into his ear. His eyes opened. He got out of bed and lifted his sister high enough for her head to punch a bowl into the ceiling.

'I'll cook us something,' he said, unloading supplies from

her arms. He felt light enough to perform single finger hand-stands.

*

XYOYX reconvened in The Queen's. Terra cotta. Morale was severely depleted. Several members were missing. Several members were missing limbs. Among the missing was the barman. Ryan and Neil took it in turns to bring trays of milk out from behind the bar. When everyone was ready, they bowed their heads and Ryan begun.

'I think we can all agree how obvious it is that the dinosaur belonged to the mayor and he sent it to eat us all.'
'Really obvious,' someone said.

'Definitely,' someone else said.

They talked at length about the need to overthrow the mayor and make the town a castle. They repeated insults. They threw balls of hair.

When Casper entered they all stood and rose onto the balls of their feet. 'Casper! You came.' A line formed and people patted Casper on the back. He was led to the head of the table and his seat pulled out for him. XYOYX straightened their necks.

'You're still doing this?' Casper asked. He stared into his milk. 'This is stupid.'

'What do you mean?'

'Now it's here, can't we all just fight the night?'

'Casper,' Ryan said, lowering his voice. 'The mayor's on the night's team. That's why he was in his bunker with everyone he knew hiding out and not getting hurt or made dead.'

'Ryan,' Casper said. 'The mayor isn't on the night's team. He was in there because he was scared of you.'

'He didn't do anything to stop it. He started it. It's his fault.'

'No, it isn't.'

'Are you on his team?'

'There aren't teams.'

Neil Vess pulled a fork from a cottage pie and thrust it through Casper's eardrum. Casper didn't retaliate. He yanked out the fork, plugged the hole with his thumb, and left. Everyone's disappearing, he thought.

He walked as fast as he could walk to City Hall. The mayor was in his office, ringed by full teapots shaped like chimpanzees. They called for cushions and built walls inside walls. They didn't sleep. They wrote notes and folded them into paper planes and threw them back and forth until there was something for tomorrow.

*

Shape didn't find what he normally found when he descended through the skylight of the house he visited most frequently. He found the Billion who never moved awake and washing dishes.

'You came,' Alec Cole said. 'I was told you'd come.'

'I haven't come,' Shape said. 'I'm not here.'

'Wonderful.'

Alec bent both of the intruder's arms behind his back and tied them with a cable tie. He did the same to the feet. He carried Shape down to the basement and arranged him in a dog basket. 'You can wait here until I decide what next.'

A,

I'm on a train to London. Drinking overpriced beer. Drawing concentric circles in a notebook. Trying to write. It's not going well. I kill characters whenever it rains. Or if I've had too much to eat. I don't know if anyone will be left by the end. I hope not.

It's been raining without stopping. There are flood warnings in seventy places. A man on a mobility scooter got washed into a river. A person died trying to take photographs of the waves.

I like wet days. I like being happier than the weather. It doesn't happen often. But sometimes. Sometimes I can touch my toes. I like that too.

Pedro's having a baby. He says it might be the quickest way to lose your selfishness. That's not why he's having it. It's just something he said. He's having it because his dog gets lonely.

Kevin called earlier. He doesn't call often. It's too expensive.

He lives somewhere warmer now. He won an award. He picks turtles out of the sand when they get stuck and throws them back into the ocean. His girlfriend wears wooden jewellery. Her name is Ione. You're supposed to say it like irony.

I asked what he remembered about Paul Highton. He laughed. He said nine and a half fingered. Maybe Kevin ripped Paul's finger off. He was mean when we were small. I remember that he cut one of your pigtails off in assembly. I remember that you didn't mind.

You were always calm. It made you seem sleepy.

Will you reply to these? Do they arrive? I'm picturing a bored satellite reading them. And laughing. Pointing down through the roof of this carriage. Telling jokes to his satellite friends,

C

Seven.

Billions:
    Full Town Think tank
    Concerning What To
    Do Next
    Voluntary
    Salmon Pink

*

Pele crawled through every room in The Burrow looking for Shape. He usually came home when the sky was olive green. Pele would wait up listening for the clack of the boat against the riverbank. The sky was tangerine.

Pele tried handstands.

He tried screaming.

And beating one hand with the other.

He'd found someone where there was supposed to be no one. Now there was just him where there was supposed to be no one. He didn't want to be just him. He wanted to be capable of handstands.

He carried on through the caverns, collapsing stacks of saucers and overturning display cases jammed with stuffed chameleons. He fought dinosaur skeletons and jumped through canvases layered with mud and spit. He cut his hands on split marbles. He punched through stained glass.

And settled in the skull of a mammoth, head clamped between his knees. Which was when he saw the small pile of things arranged in a pyramid. A wax model of a cheeseburger. A rusted microphone. A plastic tooth. They were his things. Things that had disappeared when he'd turned his back on them.

Pele climbed out of the head and ran to the kitchen. He made a breakfast of bread and ham, drank tea, washed in the canal, and changed his clothes. The canoe he'd come in was still tethered to the brass loop hammered into the bank. He untied it. He'd find Shape.

*

President Captain blinked. The remaining Billions assembled before him were sitting in complete silence. Initially, they'd taken their usual seats. But when they'd noticed the holes, everyone had relocated to form a clump near the back of the hall.

'Hello,' the mayor said. He looked above him. There was no sound engineer. 'I hope you're all okay.' He looked at Diana, perched on the heap of books, knotting her mouth in reassurance. 'I'm not.'

'Do you have a plan?' Comet asked, not loud and not needing to be. 'Please say yes.'

President Captain shook his head. 'Not yet. I know none of you are happy with me. I'm not happy with me. We called this meeting to ask what you want to do. If you have any ideas for keeping back the night and whatnot.'

A sculptor stood. 'Did anyone actually make a bunker when the aliens were coming?' He karate chopped the air as he spoke. 'I did. It's still there. I'm going to hide in my bunker. Nobody else is allowed in. If anyone tries to get in, I'll thumb out their eyes. I'm leaving now.' He left.

'I think you should listen to us more,' someone said. 'My husband fell in love with a tuna salad yesterday. Bad things are happening. Ominous omens.'

'How about we open a help desk? Casper will man it. You can ask him anything.'

'Um,' said Casper. He was sitting cross legged beside the mayor, trying not to appear present. He still felt like one long Um when faced with large crowds.

'Thank you,' said someone.

'Cowabunga,' said someone else.

'I think we should kill all the ghosts and stuff and whatever.'

'Listen, we all think that.'

'Then it's decided.'

'I think we should go and hide in The Jungle.'

'I'm not going in The Jungle. There are giant holes in there.'

'And lions!'

'We should try talking to the people above the clouds. With a megaphone or something. You should do it.'

'I can try that,' President Captain said. 'I can use the speakers on The Clock Pitch.'

'You'd better.'

'I will.'

'Well, you'd better.'

Alec Cole stood and removed the hot water bottle he'd been wearing on his head. Billions gasped. They said things like 'the mayor' and 'the better mayor' and 'I want that mayor' and so on. 'Don't worry,' he said. 'I'm not trying to be mayor again. I just want to make a suggestion.'

Diana did a thumbs up to her husband from atop the dream encyclopedias. 'I'm an ear,' President Captain said. 'We're all ears.'

'I think we should have a Tentacle Festival. As soon as possible. Isn't that what they used to be for?' The mayor thought of the book in his annex. Alec Cole had read it too. In it, The Candy King claimed that Tentacle Festivals were the only thing useful in holding back the night. To hold it back, you had to laugh at it. They were there for when things got too serious. Only The Candy King had not managed one when one was most important. The sky had been too dim. Billions had been too scared. The eruption never came.

President Captain made fists and cracked his neck, first to one side, then the other. 'Elgar,' he said. 'Begin preparing the coffee. We are going to have a Tentacle Festival.' Billions hollered and threw their chairs through the roof, leaving wide holes through which the darkening sky stared down at them.

*

In the purple light above the canopy, Avery saw something familiar in the slope of J23's face. He'd seen the same slope before. In town.

'I recognize you,' he said. 'What was your name before you came here?'

J23 didn't reply. He raised an arm and stroked the roof of feathers above them. 'Is it… are you Crispin the Great?'

'Just Crispin is fine. Don't tell anyone when we get down.'

'You died. Somewhere on the edge of town. You got really old and then you died.'

'I'm not that old.'

'Yes you are. They put a statue up of you.'

'How do I look?'

'Not hairy.'

As the faint line of the canal came into view, Avery was again distracted by what lay below them. They were riding in a wicker basket suspended below a giant rainbow parakeet. It flew long laps over the deepest Jungle, never changing speed or tipping.

'It's best to live with you. I should get everyone to move into The Jungle.'

'No.'

'Why?'

'I'll show you.'

*

Deaf Paul woke up in an abandoned lot beyond The Meatball District. There were red holes in his hands and his shoes were missing and he was damp. Angelica was standing over him, her arms flapping in worry.

'Where are the penguins?' she said. 'Where are the penguins?'

He scuttled backwards, unsure of where he was. She raised her hands, trying to explain with them that she couldn't inflict hurt even if she wanted to. 'Where,' she said very slowly. 'Are... the... penguins?'

The memory of being dismissed from the council resurfaced from the depths of Deaf Paul's head. He began sob and shake. Angelica knelt. She took a pen from the pocket of her apron. She took his arm and wrote onto it *come with me*. Then she drew a penguin.

*

Dear XYOYX,

Can we make a truce, just for The Tentacle Festival? We can call it The Tentacle Truce. Even if you don't trust me, help us try to do this,

President Captain

*

Dear President Captain,

Fine. But we don't think that's a very good name. We also don't think it will do anything to stop the night because you made the night and you are the worst. If you do any mean night related things to anyone, we'll kill and eat you,

XYOYX

*

Billions gathered on The Clock Pitch to listen to the mayor's attempt to communicate with the voices in the sky. They didn't sit in the stands. They sat in a huddle in the centre of the pitch, on blurry white lines, surrounded by the debris of broken clocks. President Captain was in the council box, trying to be a sound engineer. A fist of static jumped from the speaker system. He began to speak. Light snow fell.

*

Transcript of the Mayor's Conversation With the Voices Above the Clouds

M: Is anyone up there?

C: No.

M: Really?

C: What do you want?

M: Listen, stop sending all the scary things. You're making everyone really sad and really scared too.

Let the record show that the mayor is bouncing impatiently.

C: We can't.

A pause.

M: Why not?

Let the record show that the mayor's voice is extremely whiny and annoying right now.

C: The night is necessary. You need it.

M: We don't want it.

C: Do you want to live inside a bubble forever?

Let the record show that the mayor has turned to the billions and is conducting a vote by way of arm raising.

M: We've conferred and decided that yes, we'll take the bubble.

C: We were being rhetorical.

M: What?

C: You need to work out how to fight this.

Let the record show that the mayor just sighed into his megaphone and everyone blotted their ears and again made mention of 'the other, better mayor.'

M: How do we fight it?

C: What did we just say?

M: I don't remember.

C: We're leaving now. We're very busy.

M: Stop. Stop. Stop. Stop. Hello?

Let the record show that the mayor's nose has run down to his waist. Let the record also show that I think Alec Cole should be mayor instead of the mayor.

*

Pele stabled his canoe in the dock below the tearoom. Eliza Seuss descended the stairs to greet him. She wondered if he was a ghost. She flicked his eyeball.

'What are you doing?'

'Someone came looking for you,' she said, pressing the deposit numbers into his hand. It would have been the first time someone had returned from The Jungle. She knew he'd never reached The Jungle.

'What?'

'Someone came looking for you,' she said.

'Who?'

'The other one from the radio. The thinner one.'

'Where did he go?'

'The Jungle.' Pele's face became blank, then green, then blank again. 'You should come up for tea. Sit down. You're not a ghost. We can talk. Shape told me about you.'

Pele didn't ask anything else. He followed her up the stairs, accepted a cup of tea, and took a seat by the window, watching the weak snow flurries of snow. He focused on the moment they hit the water and died. Eliza claimed a seat two away from him. 'You know Shape?' he said, not moving his eyes.

'We talk when he comes through.'

'I didn't think he spoke to anyone.'

'He didn't. That's why we started. Then you came.'

'I didn't mean to.'

She put a finger into her tea, withdrew it, and licked it. 'He said he was scared of you because you just appeared and he had no choice. Today he said he didn't want a choice anymore.'

'Oh,' Pele said, picturing Avery being eaten.

He hadn't noticed it in The Burrow, or rowing down the canal, but the sky had noticeably dimmed. The fans of colour that used to sit behind the clouds looked as though they'd been painted over with a wash of grey slime. 'What happened to the sky?'

'I don't know. It's been getting dark. They keep talking about the night being here on the radio.'

'Did scary things happen?'

'I think so. A dinosaur ate people. People are disappearing. Shape said it didn't matter. That it wouldn't reach you two. Or that if it did, he'd kill it.'

Pele decided that he'd go first to rescue Shape, and then, unless his wife had heard anything else, head into The Jungle for Avery. He didn't know if it was the right choice. He guessed it might be.

*

'Didn't you ever wonder why there are so many buildings and so few of us?' J23 asked. They were standing on the central platform, looking out at the seemingly endless web of wooden roads that crisscrossed the trees.

'No,' Avery said. He was being honest. He hadn't thought his usual amount of thoughts since arriving.

'Come on.'

Together they walked along rope bridges, through tree houses filled with people playing cards and giving each other dead legs. They kept going. They walked further than their eyes could have seen. The birds began to look thin, and to whistle curtly, almost sarcastically. The wood of the buildings was damp and splintered. The faces hidden in the tree knots went sour.

They walked through towns of tree houses filled with piles of litter and smelling of rotten milk. The people in these houses remained unmoving in bed, curling and uncurling sporadically like caterpillars.

Crispin paused next to a person covered in white fur. 'That's what happens if you stay in The Jungle,' he said. 'The Gloom comes.'

'What?'

'They get tired. They get bored. Nowhere to go anymore, no way to leave. This is it now. This is all.'

'Then you have to go. You have to get out. Come with me.'

'I can't. My town isn't there anymore. My people aren't there. The night came and it took them.'

'So you're going to stay here and wait for this?' Crispin shrugged and looked into his feet. 'What if a horde of lions charged you out of the forest?'

'I told you there are no lions.'

'But what if there were?'

'Your town is still there. You need to go. You can leave in the morning. Whatever will happen to them will be better than this.' Avery nodded. He had to go. He didn't want to. He already felt glued to The Jungle. It would hurt. Skin would rip.

*

Complaints fielded by Casper after installing himself in City Hall behind a table fronted with a sign reading QUESTIONS? JUST ASK!

-I found my husband grated into a pile. He looked like parmesan. I didn't like it at all. Who is responsible? I think it was Ella Peti.

-A seemingly bottomless hole has appeared in our bathroom. I've lost several pairs of slippers and a toothbrush. We've been pissing into it and there's never any smell afterwards.

-How do you explain my husband's sudden refusal to participate in human pyramids?

-I'm confused. I thought you killed that dinosaur and that was it. Now there's more? Can't you just kill everything else? This is the worst. You and the mayor are the worst. XYOYX till death.

*

President Captain, Lucille Captain, Casper Font, and Kevin, sat silently in the empty milk bar, listening to mumble of the radio. They were waiting to be sleepy. Nobody was sleepy. Preparations for The Tentacle Festival had begun. If they failed, it was likely that the night would use the opportunity to eat them all. If they succeeded, maybe something would start to get better.

Kevin suggested playing Yahtzee with the set kept behind the bar. Everyone agreed. One by one they fall asleep onto their dice, until Lucille Captain had won. When they woke up, it was with rows of red squares stamped into their foreheads.

A,

I've been in London a week. I'm living with a woman who said I could live with her for nothing. She likes my books. She gives me money for wine. We drink on weekdays. Everything else on the weekends. She likes it when I read to her. I read a whole book out loud without stopping. We were in the bath. We both had nosebleeds.

The woman's name is Ellen.

She's almost double my age. But we get on.

I mostly sleep until four or five. When I wake up, I stay on the ground for at least two more hours. I catch up on the news. Not the real news. The real news is boring. I like seeing what Jennifer Lawrence is wearing when she buys coffee. Honestly. It sounds stupid. But it's comforting. I don't know why.

Ellen comes home from work at around eight. We drink beers. Watch TV. Read. Sometimes she gets a little angry at me. That's okay.

Nan called to say the dog's still alive.

Kevin called to say the turtles still get stuck.

And it's raining. I don't know why I keep saying that. You probably know. You're probably in England. Maybe Gloucester. You might live next to school. You might be engaged in an affair with Mr Cartwright.

I'm making things up.

I don't have anything to go on.

I tried searching your name. All I found was an accountant from Florida and a woman in Nebraska who makes jewellery out of coke cans,

C

Eight.

Elgar woke early and rode his Greyhound to The Brewery under a sky that was no longer any recognizable hue of red. The Brewery was a tall, copper structure on the West side of town, toward the planetarium, between the junkyard and the rice pudding fields. Already, hot balls of fog were rising from the tip of chimney. The air smelled of coffee beans and pine needles and bubblegum.

A councilman was waiting outside to take his dog. He dismounted and entered the building. Several Billions were perched like gargoyles on tall stools ringing the cauldron of coffee.

'How is it?' he asked.

'It's good,' said Comet. 'Strong. Sweet.'

'Does it taste like coffee?'

'Only a little. And when we're done, it shouldn't at all.'

'Thank you.'

He exited the Brewery and climbed back onto his Greyhound, heading for City Hall. Once there, he ordered the dog to sit, and made his way to the roof of the building. The Festival Ground. The pristine field of grass reserved only for festival use. In the centre stood a raised platform for the mayor. Around it, thick pegs hammered into the ground served as podiums for those closest to him. Elgar climbed atop the one that was his and stared into the sky. It's almost over, he thought.

*

Casper and Kevin woke up alone in the milk bar. They yawned, stretched, and pointed at the squares on each other's foreheads. Casper slid behind the bar to boil water. Kevin drew the curtains. A gloomy blackcurrant light was all the sky offered. He collected candle stubs and lit them instead.

Casper slid a tea across to Kevin. 'How do you feel?' he asked.

'Like nothing.'

Like nothing was the same way Casper felt about Tatiana. It was as though she'd never existed anywhere. He knew the reason at least. The reason he'd turned Alice into The Dream Nurse and The Dream Nurse into someone who was no longer there. 'Why?'

'It was all fake,' Kevin said. 'It was like a spell or something.'

'Isn't it supposed to be like that anyway?'

'I don't know. Maybe.'

Casper guessed a spell was something that happened to a person making them act in ways they couldn't control. He guessed that the difference was, sometimes you didn't mind that. 'What did it feel like?' he said. 'In her throat?'

'Good,' Kevin said. 'Wet. And cold.'

'Um.'

'I wish you'd done it.'

'I'm glad you did.'

They drank until their cups were empty. Kevin stood. 'Do you need a suit? I have spares.'

'It's okay, thank you. I'd like to go back home anyway. I've got one.'

'See you on the roof.'

'Okay.'

It took a full sky change for Casper to walk by to The Clay Modeling District. The usually burbling factories sat unmoving around his cardboard hill. He entered, lit a lantern, and turned on the radio, as he looked for his octopus suit.

'-is here with your guide to festival fashions. Aaron, tentacle suckers. Yes or depress?'

'With suckers I think it's how you wear them. What they're made of. How many. Personally, I find a small number of suckers, tastefully made out of crushed velvet to be a beautimous addition to any suit.'

Casper's suit was in a cereal box below his bed. He placed

it on the floor and delicately unfolded the arms and legs. The last time he'd worn it, Kevin had ripped one of the tentacles off. Diana had sewn it back on. She'd smiled and said it was no problem but had been audibly grinding her teeth.

'-finding the perfect balance between *yes, I'm here* and *everyone look at me right now*. It can be quite a war. What you really need—'

He didn't know what to feel. They were there then they weren't. Like last night, or his clock, or the tea he'd made for breakfast. There was some movement though, higher than his belly, a deep pointless swirling that felt as though it would continue indefinitely.

*

Deaf Paul woke up in a strange house with a strange woman standing over him, sucking her teeth. He looked at his arms. They were covered with instructions and drawings of penguins. The words said things like *towels under the sink* and *don't fall asleep in your clothes* and so on.

Angelica dipped her head. She turned and walked away. Deaf Paul followed her into the kitchen. The walls were obscured by framed photos of Angelica with her late husband, Dago. In the majority of the photos, the couple cradled a pair of porcelain penguins while standing before various monuments in Billion. Deaf Paul had to stoop to see them. He smiled at the dead husband. And waved.

He reached out an arm to try and help his host with the kettle but she batted it away. She liked having things to look after. Four lumps of granite lay in miniature beds in her loft. A stuffed marmoset in her living room had its waistcoat changed every nine days.

Deaf Paul made the sound he made whenever he forgot how the sounds he made sounded. Level with his eyebrows, high above Angelica's hair, the two photographed penguins had been lodged in a tight gap between the cabinet and the ceiling. He reached up and took them down. He made the sound again. 'What is it?' Angelica turned to find out.

She paused.

She rushed his knees, knotted her arms around them and squeezed so tight that he fell backwards, careful to raise his arms and save the figurines.

*

'Is your head okay?' President Captain said. He was on the duvet, wrestling with his octopus suit. As he inserted his legs, the tentacles cackled with stress. 'It looks bad.'

'It's not your fault. It's okay.' Neither of them thought it was okay. A flap of bone had been punched inward, exposing a slab of brain. Juice from the pink meat ran from the hole and down her face. Lucille dabbed at her cheek with a handkerchief.

They both knew why that night had featured violent dreams. It was because of Alec Cole. The mayor didn't dislike Alec Cole. He was afraid of him. He thought himself a worse mayor, with less impressive shoulders and an inability to vocally project. If Alec Cole hadn't spontaneously climbed into bed and refused to climb out, the mayor would never have become the mayor.

'I got fat,' President Captain said, examining himself in the mirror. 'I don't even look like a real octopus. I look like a walrus dressed as an octopus.'

Lucille rested her leaking head on his shoulder. 'You don't look like a walrus. You're just growing.'

'I don't want to grow.'

'I don't want you to grow either.' They looked at each other in the mirror, Lucille leaning on President Captain, President Captain with his hand around her waist. 'I like Casper,' she said. 'And Kevin. And last night.'

'I think I was mean to Casper. I shouldn't have kept telling him what to do.'

'He likes you. He's helping you.'

'He's helping everyone.'

'I like Casper.'

'Me too.'

*

The L were gathered on their central platform to see Avery off. It had been decided that leaving The Jungle on foot was impossible. He'd inevitably turn around because the tree houses would always be closer. Instead, J23 had decided that the only suitable method for getting him home was flying. He'd head towards the town beneath a parakeet and parachute down beside the canal.

The Jungle had become so dark that irrespective of the time the candles in the mason jars were lit. The L were used to this. Things were light. Then they got dark. Then they got darker. Then they went light again. To compensate, thick candles had been melted into the bird's wings and mirrors sewn into the basket.

'Bye,' Avery said. 'Thanks for letting me go on your bird thing.'

'See you never.'

U228 plucked a feather from the parakeet and it bucked into the air, beginning the long flight back to Billion.

*

Though long since lost in the swamp, the original intention of The Tentacle Festival was to act as a barrier against the night. If ghosts are laughed at, they leave. It was thought that regular festivals held the colour in the sky, locked the hands above the clouds and made the gods mute. A successful festival is judged by whether or not a collective levitation is achieved

following The Tentacle Dance.
> We couldn't do it.
> We tried.
> We're dying.
> All Hail The Candy King.

*

On the roof of City Hall, Billions had noticed the new spaces that had appeared, and were running in weird orbits of the mayor's mound to fill them. Despite a severe reduction in the number of attendees since the last Tentacle Festival, the number of stalls and volume of coffee had doubled.

Casper arrived late and in sunglasses. He spotted Kevin, flanked by two four year olds, eating chicken strips at the tattoo stand. 'Do you like my tattoo?' He gestured at a red scrawl on his bicep. 'It's a lobster.'

'Um.'

Kevin shook off his companions. He lifted two mugs of coffee from the grass, passed one to Casper, and led him away. 'The mayor says we have to stand on stumps.'

'I don't want to dance up there. People will look at us.'

'That's the point. Come on.'

They shouldered their way through the hyperactive crowd, gulping mugs of coffee. Casper looked up at the near empty council ring. 'Isn't there anyone else left on the council?'

'Just Elgar and Comet.'

The air horn sounded.

'Quick.'

Billions fixed their suits, licked smudges from each other's noses, and took places around the central mound. Casper grudgingly swung himself up onto one of the bollards around the mayor and finished his coffee.

The air horn sounded again.

President Captain raised his tentacles to the sky. 'Billions,' he said. 'The sky is dark and we're all really scared and there's a lot to be really scared of. There's also a lot we don't have to be scared of. For example, Casper Font, Kevin, my wife Lucille, warm milk, origami, trying new things, and most types fish.'

'Butternut squash,' someone shouted.

'Hugs,' someone else shouted.

'Where?' someone asked.

'Exactly,' said the mayor. He picked out his wife. She was standing by a stall that sold small piñata punch bags filled with blocks of fudge. She attempted a salute and slapped herself in the eyes with an octopus leg. 'I'd like to say thank you to XYOYX for agreeing to The Tentacle Truce and being here with us today. I'm glad, even if it's just for now, that we could put our differences behind us.'

Neil Vess turned around and Ryan Vess knocked him over. 'We still think you did it,' Ryan shouted.

'I'd like to thank The Candy King for his help. I'd like to thank DI Dolo and my most trusted councilman Elgar. I'd like to thank coffee. And I'd like to thank everyone else for not killing me yet. I don't know if this will work. I don't know if we'll succeed. But we're trying.'

'Hurry up.'

'President Suckhole.'

People cheered. The coffee in their heads made them loud and twitchy.

'Does everyone have a mug?' Billions raised their coffees and yelled that they did. 'Okay,' the mayor said. He emptied his mug in one swallow and hurled it over his shoulder. 'Go.'

The sound of smashing pottery became the only sound. As it faded, it was replaced with the same uncontrollable laughter that accompanied anyone doing The Tentacle Dance. They bent back their necks and flapped their tentacles desperately like broken scales, spinning in accelerating circles.

Kevin and Casper lashed each other's legs from across their podiums like gladiators. The mayor jabbed Elgar between the eyes then fell flat on his front, laughing and barrel-rolling down his mound. Comet leapt at the distracted Elgar, who fell too, landing on the mayor's back. They both stood and continued the dance.

Left tentacle.

Right tentacle.

Both tentacles.

Spin.

Casper paused to look into the sky. He didn't know if it was his imagination but it looked as though colours were bleeding back in, congregating to watch the madness of hysterical Billions. He looked down at his feet and saw that they were floating an inch from the ground. Deaf Paul knocked him sideways.

*

Pele woke late. Eliza Seuss hadn't thought it necessary for him to be up early. Tentacle Festival usually begun in the middle of the day and continued until everyone was asleep. The radio told her it had only recently begun.

He ambled down the stairs and sat down to a breakfast she'd made for him, already laid out at the seat he'd taken the day before. She'd guessed he'd chosen it for the view it afforded of The Jungle. He could watch and wait and hope that his friend appeared before he left.

Pele poured tea and spread lime marmalade onto thick toast. Eliza loitered behind him. He could feel her impatient warmth. Nothing stirred between the trees. 'Why are you here?' he asked, his mouth full. 'And why are you helping me?'

She took a step back. The embarrassment made it feel as though she was shrinking. 'I'd like to leave,' she said. 'This was my inheritance. I have to stay. And I help because then I get to feel involved. In some way. Somehow. I like hearing about the town.'

'You should come.'

'Here's the address.' She placed a folded square of paper next to his cup. 'I doubt the trains are running so you can just follow the black rail up to Mont Station and walk from there. I hope you find him.' She left the room.

Pele finished his food, rinsed his plate in the sink behind the counter, and walked the dirt road into town.

Everything was how Eliza had said it would be. Deserted. He'd never seen it look so dead and felt glad he'd not been there to watch the people spill out. The cobbles hadn't been cleared. Old cogs of food and small dead things rotted between them. Windows had been boarded shut. Fire had gutted a restaurant he'd once remained in for three days due to heavy snow.

The black train line was mud-caked. He walked carefully between the rails, doubting they were on, but not certain enough to feel safe. Gradually, as he neared The Circle, City Hall came into view, and with it the crew of Billions dancing fitfully on its roof. He wondered if they'd succeeded. From the light of the sky he guessed yes.

He clambered onto the platform at Mont Station and opened the map he'd been given. It was close. Two streets. Two more vacant, broken streets of frowning houses. He walked nervously, not knowing what he would do if confronted.

It was a large-double fronted house. It had never been possible to extract Alec Cole from the house of the mayor so they'd simply left him in it and written the title on another building, one closer to City Hall. Pele knocked. No answer. The door was unlocked. He pushed it open.

'Marco?' he shouted. His shoes left clear brown stamps on the carpet. 'Marco?'

'Polo.'

'Marco?'

'Polo.'

He sighed and the tension in his head fell out of his nose. The sound was coming from below him. It was unmistakably Shape. 'Marco?'

'Polo.'

A sharp punch to an exposed rectangle of floorboard opened the basement. Shape was flailing uselessly in the dog basket. 'Marco?'

'Polo.'

Pele bit the cable ties open and held Shape from behind on the warm fur. 'He is getting out of the bed,' Shape said. 'The not moving man is moving.'

'It's okay.'

'The voices I heard them again when you are not here.'

Shape twisted his arm awkwardly backwards and slid a finger into Pele's nostril. Pele reached forward and reciprocated. A deafening crash cracked the air between them.

*

'Happy Tentacle Festival, Billion. You're listening to Nine FM with me, Keira Mary-Kate. I should probably be tired. But coffee, coffee, coffee. It's here. This time of the time again. Hello to everyone on the roof of City Hall. Hello to everyone who's not.

Call, write, send us drawings of yourselves in your outfits. We'll pick a winner and send them on an all expenses paid cruise aboard the SS Pillowtalk. You have until olive green to get them. Don't forget!

Unfortunately, I couldn't be at the festival ground today because someone has to be in The Globe, flipping the switches and taking the calls. Luckily, our field reporter Milo is up there with you all now. Milo, can you hear me?'

'Hi Keira. I'm here.'

'What's the atmosphere like?'

'It's actually good this time. It's like… people are happy and stuff. I don't think I'm in danger. No one is bleeding. This is the least scary thing so far.'

'Glad to hear it. How far in to the festival are they?'

'It's been a full sky change. New coffee is being brought up.'

'There had been worries that the levitation would be unachievable because of everything that's been happening recently. How is it going?'

'Everyone looks like they're floating a bit.'

'That's wonderful. How does everyone look?

. . . .

Milo, how does everyone look?

. . . .

Milo?'

'That's it I quit.'

'What? What's happening?'

'This job is the worst job ever and I'm never doing it again and I'm going home.'

'What's happened?'

'What's happened is that a massive rock just fell out of the sky and crushed loads of people and there's a huge hole and people are falling into it and I'm going goodbye.'

'Milo?

. . .

Milo are you there?'

'Is this on? Is this turned on?'

'It's on. Who is this? Where's Milo?'

'Milo is dead. This is your mayor. I want you to know that I had nothing to do with this. I am not on their side. This wasn't me.'

*

When the first rock fell it crushed nine people. Six more plunged through the hole in the roof. Ryan and Neil Vess immediately undressed and jumped from the building, breaking their feet and somersaulting into City Hall.

'Where's the mayor?' Kevin asked Casper as they cut each other out of their suits with a penknife Kevin kept in his sock. The sky thundered.

'I don't know.' He pointed to the clouds. 'Look.'

'Stop doing that dance,' a voice from nowhere boomed. 'Sit still.'

Two hands broke through the blue ceiling. They were bigger than the last hand had been. They picked up Kimya Cole, who had been trying to haul her brother from the hole, slipped a finger into each of her cheeks, and turned her inside out. Reversed, she was a dripping chandelier of pink meat.

The hands dropped her over Angelica, who started to suffocate. Deaf Paul beat the corpse that covered her with his fists until blood freckled his nose.

'The mayor,' Kevin shouted, pointing toward the edge of the roof. Casper followed and they found him, unconscious and with a microphone in his hand. A shrill voice continued to issue from the headphones attached to it. They lifted President Captain and carried him away from the hands.

Rocks continued to fall.

Corners of the building gave up.

Bodies flattened.

'Stop moving,' the voice above the clouds screamed. 'You're all so exhausting and you're all dead too.'

This time the hands selected Elgar from the mass of people. One pinched him firmly around the waist, while the ring finger of the other broke through his teeth and continued on into his body. He looked like a boa constrictor eating a child. He screamed so hard without making any noise that the corners of his mouth tore upward and a new smile spread over his face. The finger exited the other side of his body. He went limp.

'He's so heavy,' Kevin said. 'Can't you kill it? Like you did last time.'

They'd reached a locked hatch and were attempting to unlock it using the circle of keys attached to the mayor's belt. Every key looked the same. 'That was a dinosaur,' Casper said. 'This isn't a dinosaur. It's a massive hand.'

'You're all going to shush for a while now,' said the voice. 'You're all going to disappear.'

The hands chose Casper next. They hoisted him from the hatch and dangled him by his left foot. Kevin rifled threw the mayor's pockets and threw whatever he could find. A bottle opener shaped like a wishbone. Two sewing needles. A glass eye. Nothing helped. 'Let him go. Put him down. He's a dinosaur hunter. He'll eat you.'

The free hand took Casper's arm. Casper closed his eyes and prepared to become two hunks of estranged flesh. He wondered if there would be a window of time after the split when his head continued to work. He guessed yes. He tried to write his last words. *I am the worst person in the world and I need your help.* He wanted to be thrown higher than the clouds. He wanted to glimpse Alice above them.

'Get lost, stupid hands,' Avery screamed, as the parakeet tore into Casper's captor. It bit at the bays between the giant fingers and waterfalls of blood rained down over the grass, rocks, and mushed bodies.

'Stop it,' the voice said. 'I'll crush you.'

'Try,' screamed Avery. The parakeet tugged a fingernail free and it spiraled to the ground like a sycamore key. Kevin had unlocked the hatch. He jumped through and caught the mayor's body as Casper knocked it down.

A,

I wish you'd reply. I know you don't owe me anything. But I feel dumb. I feel like I'm breaking into your house. Putting you through the trouble of having to delete these.

It's heavy weather here now. Ellen kept asking me to hug her. Then kiss her. She wanted me to sleep with her. She said I had to leave if I didn't. I did once. I didn't the next time. She broke a computer.

I didn't mind.

It was her computer.

But I lost a story I'd been working on. It was about the last two surviving members of a species called Kikimots. Kikimots look like cats except bigger and without fur. In the story, the mum Kikimot and the son Kikimot have to make it all the way across Russia. To a centre someone said would help them. Spoiler alert but the centre is really just a lab. And they get put in glass boxes and made to breed with each other repeatedly until they die.

Oh, Ellen got run over by a car last week. She didn't die.

Anyway, I've been sleeping where I can. I have friends. I have two friends. And I sleep better on their sofas than in real beds. But I'm a burden. Maybe I should go home. It's hard to tell.

Ellen keeps asking me to go back to her. I don't think I will. I think that's over now.

Leti keeps sending me photos of her boobs. I keep sending them back.

Kevin's coming to England in a couple of weeks.

Pedro's alive.

If you want to type anything in reply, please do. Anything. You can just type 'unsubscribe', if that's what you want,

C

Nine.

'You're listening to Nine FM with Pele Marti—'

'And Avery Vitafit. The sky is currently very grey, there are six hundred clouds, and I'd recommend wearing trousers.'

'Before starting, we'd like to apologise to Keira Mary-Kate for having to cover for us over the past however long it's been. It's greatly appreciated, both by ourselves and the citizens of Billion.'

'We've both been away due to personal reasons. But we're back now.'

'Avery's personal reason is that he thought I was in The Jungle so he went in there looking for me and got kidnapped by a hairy gang. It was my fault and I know that and I'm sorry.

'Pele's personal reason is that he panicked and that's okay.'

They both realized for the first time that there were no arms frantically waving from behind the glass. No one was telling them to stay on track. They didn't have a producer anymore. 'We'd also like to say to our late producer—'

'Sorry you died.'

'And to field reporter Milo Almond—'

'You died doing what you loved.'

'Our top story today concerns the events of the recent Tentacle Festival. Following a promising start and successful collective levitation, boulders began to rain from the sky as two disembodied hands cut short the lives of many of our most loved citizens.'

'This has been called by some—'

'By us—'

'The pinnacle of the night, the end of everything, and a clear indication that certain death is certain, respectively.'

'We got on the roof and looked around and it looks like almost everyone is dead. A representative from the mayor's office has asked us to let you know that any survivors will be welcomed into his bunker below City Hall. They have blankets, food, and a pinball machine.'

'For those of you who don't know, significant portions of the town's roads and rivers are now seemingly bottomless black holes. We advise against investigating these. We advise against almost everything at the present moment.'

'Neither of us know what's happening or has happened or will happen.'

'But it looks like this might be our last broadcast.'

'It's too dangerous to come back here.'

'We're going to leave the answering machine against the microphone, so that if you have anything to say, the recording will cut out, and you can say it.'

'We hope to see some of you wherever this ends.'

'Pele Marti.'

'Avery Vitafit.'

'Bye everyone.'

*

Shape was teaching Kelis how to make pizza. He was showing her how to roll out the dough and how to throw it, spinning it into the correct size and shape.

'You are too much scared when you throw,' he said. She threw the circle of dough in the air and it landed on her head. He laughed. 'You are being a stupid.'

Avery and Pele entered. They were whistling. They took their seats at the dining table and beat their cutlery against the wood. 'Slower, please,' said Shape. 'Your wife, she is not so much cooking.'

They ate while imagining their own ends. Pele saw something violent. Avery pictured blankness advancing until it erased him. Kelis felt her skin burn away.

'We should move to City Hall soon,' Avery said.

'We have to tidy first. I'm not leaving the house like this.'

'Are we having to?' asked Shape. 'Here it is nice.' Pele squeezed his hand so hard the knuckles popped.

'It seems safer. And maybe they have a plan.'

'What plan could there be?' Kelis asked.

'I don't know.'

They finished every slice of pizza and stood in a row in the kitchen, washing, drying and passing plates into cupboards.

*

'This is definitely proof,' Ryan Vess said. 'Everything that has ever happened was the mayor's fault. He tricked us into The Tentacle Truce and then he tried to kill us.'

'Yes please,' said Neil, eating something he'd found inside his bellybutton and scratching one foot with the other. It was dark in The Queen's. There was no more milk. 'Naughty mayor.'

They were the last remaining members of XYOYX. Ryan hadn't noticed. Neil had noticed but he deemed it not to be of any significance. He was still mostly interested things that came out of his body and also aliens.

'And Casper's on his side. Maybe Casper was on his side the whole time. Working against us.'

'Great.'

'We need to show them. Pass me the phone.'

*

Hello. This is XYOYX. There are a million of us and we are all really strong and we are going to kill you if you don't leave. We will eat all of you. Not the bones. We will make soup with the bones though. We know what you did, Mayor Suckbutts. Leave the town. The town belongs to us now.

*

Following The Tentacle Festival, the town of Billion effectively went into shutdown. Government employees quit. All bars, restaurants, and shops were closed or abandoned. The remaining Billions aligned themselves neither with the mayor nor XYOYX. They saw the holes that spotted the streets and barricaded themselves inside their homes. They did not turn on their radios. They built pillow castles and made pyramids from their remaining food. None of them would leave their homes again. They would cower in cabinets as their floorboards were sucked into the earth.

*

A chalkboard had been erected in the mayor's bunker. They had taken turns to write ideas on it. Casper had written *dress up like hands so they think we're them and then leave us alone.* The mayor had written *metal suits with guns as arms.* Comet had drawn a picture of a cat with wheels instead of legs.

Every pillow, blanket, and chair had been brought downstairs. It had become a place impossible to injure yourself in. 'It's obvious, isn't it,' Comet said, falling into a beanbag and puncturing a carton of juice with a straw.

'Yes,' Casper said.

'No,' the mayor said.

'We have to leave town. We can't stay here. They'll keep attacking it until nothing is left. They won't stop.'

'What if they do stop?'

The door swung open. 'They won't stop.' Avery entered with Pele, Kelis, and Shape. They were carrying tins of food and bottles of milk. 'I met Crispin the Great in The Jungle. He said they just carry on and carry on until everything's gone. No one survives. That's why we're almost all the same age.'

'You came,' the mayor said. 'Someone came.'

'You saw Crispin the Great?' Casper asked, not wanting an answer and not getting one. He felt travelsick. His ship was listing.

The new arrivals set down their possessions and found places in the landscape of cushions. Pele positioned himself in Shape's lap. Kelis lay with her head on Avery's stomach. 'We thought you might have a plan,' he said.

'We almost do.'

'We don't.'

'What is it?'

'We're going to leave.'

'And go where?'

No one said anything. They all thought the same thought. 'The West Wall.

Can we get through it?'

'This is possible,' said Shape. 'I have seen many blind bird going through.'

'Well, we have to try. If we get through, and block up our entrance, they won't know where we are. They won't be able to find us.'

'Someone should go first. On an albatross. And check that it's possible to get through. If we all go at once it might be conspicuous.' Everyone stared at Comet. 'Don't worry,' he said. 'I said it because I wanted to volunteer. I don't really know any of you that well and it's kind of boring down here.'

'I want to get Ryan and Neil,' Casper said.

'They won't come. If they do it, will be to eat me in my sleep.'

'I'll convince them.'

'Fine. But be quick. There are new holes opening all the time.'

Casper nodded. He walked through to the lobby where the bodies had been stacked and sawed off Elgar's hand using Kevin's penknife.

*

Diana had seen everything she could see in the ceiling. She went into the bathroom. Sixteen's body was festering on the rug. Black soil had leaked from his skin, forming an outline around his shape. She pulled him down the stairs by his ankle. As he came, fingers and ears snagged and dropped away. She took him to the garden and set him on fire.

The flames burned black and blue.

They rose higher than the house and made sounds like corn kernels popping.

She considered jumping onto the fire and crawling inside her dead husband and falling asleep. She made herself promise not to be melodramatic.

*

Ryan and Neil were sitting behind the bar when Casper got to The Queen's. They were playing a version of Snap that involved slapping the other person instead of claiming the cards.

Ryan jumped up. Neil slapped his thigh.

'We're leaving town,' Casper said.

'It worked! The town is ours!'

'You should come with us.'

'No way.' Ryan folded his arms. Neil looked from Casper to Ryan then folded his arms too. 'The mayor is going to kill you.'

'The mayor didn't do it.'

'How do you know?'

'Elgar died.'

'Really?'

'Yes really.' Casper put Elgar's hand on the table. Neil instinctively picked it up and wiggled it in the air before his brother's face. 'Ryan, let's paint it green and pretend it's an alien hand.'

'Put it down, Neil. I don't like it.'

Neil was confused. 'It's a hand,' he said.

'I know what it is. That's why I don't like it.'

'Oh.'

Casper sat. 'The mayor almost died too. Me and Kevin had to rescue him. Then Avery had to rescue us.'

'Are you sure?'

'I was there.'

'You think we should come with you?'

'You can't stay here.'

They engaged in a clumsy hug. Neil latched himself to their shoulders, wetting their shirts with his eyes. 'We're really sorry for everything,' Ryan said. 'We just wanted you out of jail.'

'You're the best,' said Neil.

'I know. Thank you. You tried.'

'We did try hard.'

'I know you did.'

'You're the best.'

He helped them pack what few things they had left, issued them each with a blue-burning lantern, and led them to City Hall.

*

The mood in the bunker below City Hall was buoyant. Nobody knew why. It felt fragile. They were all trying their best not to drop anything in case it broke. Shape and Kelis had made confetti from old newspapers.

'Surprise!' they shouted as the door opened. Each threw handfuls of paper squares into the air.

'Oh,' Neil said. 'I feel like a bride.'

'Shut up, Neil,' said Ryan.

'This is the happiest day of my life.'

Several pots of tea were made and the radio was turned

on. Everyone half-listened, while playing games on the ground or talking about what they would find beyond The West Wall. Shape thought dogs. Lucille thought oceans.

The answering machine had been set to interrupt the wildebeest recording whenever it received anything new. Nobody noticed, but a call did come in. In the message, a person asked, in a whisper, what City Hall was and where she might find it.

Diana arrived to another confetti welcoming committee. She'd brought Eliza Seuss with her. She'd found Eliza Seuss looking almost dead by The Turpentine Stream. Shape fussed. He heaped so many blankets over her head that she couldn't move. Instead, she crumpled to the ground and quietly acclimatized to the sudden mess of people.

It was decided that they should play bulldogs to ensure drowsiness. President Captain was the first dog. He stood in the centre of the room as his last citizens ran in waves past him, from behind one line to behind the other. The rules dictated that he was to knock whoever he could down and have them switch to his side, but for the first three runs he didn't move. He stared at them and laughed. There were no giant hands in his head.

Pele was the first to be caught.

Lucille the last.

They started again.

They played like this until everyone was either blue or unconscious. Aching and half-asleep, they sat around a pyramid of torches, trying to keep their eyes open, grateful that they still had the option.

'We should say something about everyone who died,' the mayor said.

'What should we say about them?'

'We should say that we wished they hadn't died.'

A,

I'm on a plane again. Sitting next to Kevin. He convinced me to come with him. To The Maldives. I don't know where The Maldives is. I'm afraid to look at a map.

We were sitting outside a pub in Soho. It was lunchtime. He asked me if I was okay. I said I was okay. I asked if he was okay. He rolled up his sleeves to show his arms. They were the colour of tangerines. He said he was okay too.

We drank until it got dark. He told me about Ione. How she never did anything wrong. But that didn't mean he wanted her to stay. He said she didn't like to touch the turtles. That she flinched.

I told him about Ellen. And Spain. I was being embarrassing. I was crying loudly. Like a toddler. He played Candy Crush on his phone until I was done.

We went to a park on the hill where we used to live. Drank more beers. Smoked cigarettes. Waited for the people who own dogs to turn up with the sun. We talked about school. About you. About Tatiana. He knew where most people had ended up. I don't know how. He knew that Paul lived alone in Glasgow. He knew that Maura taught English in Tokyo.

He told me I should go back with him. He'd break up with Ione. I could help with the turtles. I said okay. I had a little money from the Spanish edition of my last book thanks to Pedro and I had six t-shirts thanks to him too.

So now we're on a plane. I don't know how long the journey is. We were drinking at the airport. Kevin's asleep. He's snoring. The woman next to him keeps rolling her eyes.

I won't ask you anymore questions.

I'm sorry, I'm still here,

C

Ten.

A pot of porridge was on the fire when everyone woke up. They yawned and stretched and kicked off their blankets. Shape was bounding in circles, wielding his wooden spoon like a sword.

'It's a morning,' he shouted. 'I am cooking.'

They took it in turns to splash themselves at the sink then took bowls and ladled breakfast into them. When everyone had eaten, President Captain wiped clean the chalkboard and called everyone to quiet.

'We have to work out the plan,' he said. 'The real plan.' He drew two horizontal lines across the board in pink chalk.

'What's that?' Ryan asked.

'It's the wall,' said the mayor. 'How do we get to it?'

'We can go on The Pillow Talk,' said Pele. 'I drove it once, when no one was looking. It's anchored just up from the tearoom. And the captain got eaten ages ago.'

'Good. Great. We'll go on that.' He drew a boat with an arrow pointing toward the wall. 'We also need to find enough food to sustain us forever. There's what we have here, and we could bring the dinosaur body if we want to but I don't think we really want to.'

'We could kill and salt some of the albatrosses,' Avery suggested. 'Albatross jerky.'

'It is okay,' Shape said. 'In my home is much food. We pick it up en the route.'

'This is boring,' said Neil. 'I'm bored.'

The mayor ignored him. He drew a wonky drawing of Shape's face on the board and put a tick beside it. 'We'll need weapons too. To break through the wall. I doubt Comet's got far, if anywhere.'

'I have a bazooka,' said Neil. He held his hands out ahead of him and made explosion sounds, spraying spit onto a half-asleep Kelis.

'Stop it, Neil.'

Neil returned his imaginary bazooka to his pocket. 'I'm bored,' he said defiantly.

'Aren't there police things?' Casper asked. 'Didn't they have clubs or guns or something?'

'They took everything when they quit. I asked someone for his baton back and he kept hitting me in the neck with it.'

A clicking sound came from the door. It was the albatross pecking. Lucille let it in. A piece of paper with a note on it was tied to the bird's foot. President Captain unrolled it and read out loud. 'The wall was made of Styrofoam. I made a big hole already. When are you coming? I'm bored. By the way, there's only unending blackness behind it.'

*

Everything was packed into trailers queued up behind the door. The sky was almost fully black. Only six fat clouds glowed with trapped light.

It had been decided that the use of vehicles would be too dangerous. New holes were opening spontaneously. It would be two easy to lose everyone all at once.

They shuffled anxiously along the streets and around the black circles that populated them. No houses were lit. There were no other sounds.

Halfway through Little Uganda, a sound like a rock hitting water happened. The chain of people came to a halt.

'Did we lose someone?' President Captain asked.

'We lost someone,' Diana told him.

'No we didn't,' said Ryan.

Pele raised his hand. 'I just saw someone fall through a hole.'

They all looked at each other and shook their shoulders. 'It was Eliza,' Shape said.

'Who?'

'Eliza. She owns the tearoom.'

'That's who that was?'

'Who what was?'

'Who are we talking about?'

'Someone disappeared.'

'Who disappeared?'

'Someone called Eliza.'

'Who's Eliza?'

'I'm pretty sure no one disappeared.'

'I can't see anyone that's disappeared.'

'Hurry up,' said the mayor. 'And be quiet. Come on.'

As Casper walked, he wondered if he'd be forgotten so quickly. He wondered if being forgotten so quickly mattered. He guessed not.

*

In quiet darkness, The SS Pillow Talk glided down the canal. Casper was the only person not below deck. He stood under the fairy lights, watching feet kick the houses of Billion through clouds as hunks of rock tumbled through roofs. He jumped when he noticed Lucille Captain approach.

'Sorry,' she said. She placed her hands and chin on the railing. In the distance, The Globe shattered into bites of hail. 'We left at the right time.'

'Everyone else will be dead.'

'Maybe.'

'We should have done something. We should have gotten them to come.'

'They wouldn't have come. They wouldn't leave their houses. They'll find their own ways to wherever they need to be.'

Casper sank into a cross legged sit. 'Will there be anything else?' he said. 'There's probably nothing behind the wall.'

'We can make something behind the wall.'

'Whatever we make will be a bad copy of Billion. Everything will be smaller and darker and more empty.'

'Maybe,' Lucille said. 'It's better than nothing.'

'Everything is better than nothing. Nightmares are better than nothing. Severed cow heads are better than nothing. Melted ice cream and dog eyes and green beef are all better than nothing.'

The tangle of hot air that his words made evaporated into the black. Lucille made a quiet, low sound. 'Do you want me to go?' she said.

'No.' He stood up. 'I'm really sorry for being loud. I guess we should go inside. What are they doing?'

'We should stay outside for a little longer. Shape is teaching my husband how to dance.'

*

The SS Pillow Talk docked at The Burrow and its crew formed a line to act as a conveyor belt along which food could be passed to the ship. Avery declined to participate. He told President Captain that his stomach felt like a Ferris wheel. He waited until all eyes were elsewhere, pocketed six candles, a box of matches and a spool of string, and climbed into a lifeboat hanging from the side of the ship facing The Jungle.

Across the water, he dragged the boat onto land. He fixed pieces of string to the candles so that they would catch light when their wicks had burned halfway down, and he lead the pieces of string around tree trunks and tied them there. He lit the candles. He climbed back into the lifeboat and returned to the ship.

*

They would all usually have been in deep sleeps at the time they reached the barren plane of mud that bordered the wall.

Comet was doing star jumps with turned on torches in each of his hands. He screamed quicker and I'm hungry and so on at the hull until it was pressed against his stomach.

'You took a long time,' he said. 'It's boring here.'

'We're here now,' the mayor said. 'We should have a party.'

'A We'll Never Be Here Again Party.'

The party consisted of milk, biscuits, tag, slaps, jumps, hopscotch, marshmallows, pillows, singing, spitting, hitting, kissing, licking, tripping, pretending to be doctors, pretending to be firemen, pretending to be tigers, a kangaroo court, taking it in turns to drive the boat, and quiet time.

It lasted a long time.

Casper and Diana both eventually found themselves wandering out of the group and sitting by the canal. A fire burned in the distance. 'What's that?' Casper said. It was very obviously a fire. He was trying to make conversation.

'I don't know.'

'Oh.'

They bit their fingernails.

'I'm sorry for always being mean,' Diana said. She took a deep breath. 'It's just that you never did anything. I was worried that he would stop doing things.'

'I never had anything to do. I was a dinosaur hunter and there weren't any dinosaurs.'

'So you made one?'

'I guess.' It wasn't true but true didn't matter anymore. What mattered was keeping each other warm and preventing possible outbreaks of shouting.

'Are we friends?' Diana said.

'Do you want to be?'

'Yes please.'

They hugged. They pulled apart. 'I miss Sixteen,' Diana said. 'And I don't really know what that means.'

'Me too,' Casper said.

Back by the wall, the remaining Billions crowded round the hole, directing their torch beams into it. There was nothing for the light to pick out.

'What is it?' Ryan asked.

'I don't know,' said the mayor.

A,

We're in the Maldives. Where are you?

It's hot here.

That's obvious.

Beer is cheap. Cigarettes are cheap. Everything is slow. When people speak it sounds like singing. My shoulders look like raw steaks. We nap after lunch.

Kevin broke up with Ione. I could hear it through my bedroom wall. He asked her why she didn't like touching the turtles. She said they were gross. She said they felt like food. He asked her why she always talked about food. She asked if he was calling her fat.

I masturbated then fell asleep.

Every argument is the same argument. I'm not you, one person shouts. I'm not you, the other person shouts back. They don't make much sense to me. But that's okay. Other things do.

You should come and visit us. It's funny here. There's sand. Beer. Books. It feels like this is the only place that exists,

C

Eleven.

The town was flat when they woke up. There was no Globe. No City Hall. No Clock Pitch. The air was dark and sharp. Comet lit a fire and everyone sat in a circle, toasting bread rolls, scratching their eyes, and trying to get warm. The Wall loomed over them as they ate.

Everything was packed into three trailers. The fire was squashed out. Torches were turned on. The remaining Billions congregated at their door into the wall.

'Shotgun not going first,' said Neil.

Everybody echoed him.

Except President Captain. 'I was going to go first anyway,' he said. 'I'm the mayor.'

'The mayor of what?'

The mayor of nowhere grunted and stumbled into the darkness, lugging a trailer along behind him. The others followed.

'I think we should go that way,' said Neil, pointing to one side.

'Why?'

'It's pretty.'

There was nothing for their torches to illuminate. Beyond the wall was only blackness. It was as though they were walking through dark water. Treading carefully, they walked straight ahead. Diana had tied her left foot to a trailer. Ryan Vess had tied himself to Neil Vess.

*

A path of glowing pebbles appeared. They shrugged at each other. They followed it until a doorway in a red brick wall, blocked by a rusted portcullis.

'Hi,' said the guard. He was wearing a lion suit. 'Do you want to go through?'

'It depends,' said the mayor. 'What's on the other side?'

'More path. Some blackness. I don't really know.'

'Do we have to do anything?'

'You have to play sleeping lions. I don't know why, but not coming last in that means you're allowed to pass. Whoever comes last, has to stay on this side. Unless they fight and kill me, which they won't be able to do because I am a martial arts expert and have the reflexes of a light switch.'

'Can we confer?'

'If you want to.'

They formed a huddle and attempted to confer. The conference was not productive. Casper didn't think there was any use in getting through a gate when they didn't know what was on the other side. Lucille thought that was the best type of gate to get through. Kevin wanted to overpower the guard. The mayor wanted to play sleeping lions.

It was put to a vote.

It was decided that they would stay and play sleeping lions.

'Great,' said the guard. 'I suppose you know the rules. Everyone has to lie face down on the floor. The first person to move loses. Get into bed, baby lions.'

*

Shape lost. He didn't fully understand the concept of the game. He copied everyone else when they hit the floor, then proceeded to excavate balls of lint from his bellybutton.

'I am a stupid,' Shape said. 'I am not going also through the gate.'

'Goodbye.'

'Goodbye.'

'Goodbye.'

'Goodbye.'

'Goodbye.'

'Goodbye.'

'I'm going with you,' Pele said. 'We can find a patch of blackness and sleep until all of this is over.'

Avery pushed his nose against the nose of his best friend. They didn't move their mouths. With their eyes they said *whatever is happening is happening and something else will happen afterwards.*

*

As the remaining members of the party stepped through the gate, Comet's eyes narrowed and reddened. He felt the desire to walk drain out of him like sewage. He stared at the mayor. The mayor asked him what he was staring at.

'You,' he said. 'You're the worst and you're an idiot and I hate you.'

Neil Vess did a thumbs up. President Captain recoiled.

'What's wrong?' said the mayor.

'You're what's wrong.' He haymakered President Captain in the eyeball. 'I'm going to kill you. You're not a mayor. You're a nothing.'

The mayor cowered on the invisible floor. Ryan and Neil each gripped one of Comet's arms and held him back. 'Why are you doing this?' President Captain asked.

'Because you think you're so amazing being the mayor of a town that you let die. You became mayor by accident. No one ever liked you.'

'You're being really mean.'

Comet lashed out with a foot and caught President Captain in the mouth, knocking out three milk teeth and a three day old wad of blackcurrant bubblegum. Before his face, he made a fan with his hands. His assailant slumped forward, collapsing on President Captain's legs. A thin needle protruded from the back of his neck. The guard stood behind him, grinning.

'There's always one,' said the guard.

'One what?'

'Just one.'

'Listen,' said President Captain. 'We're going to go now. Thanks for all the help.'

*

Casper heard the rumble of footsteps in the distance grow louder. He wondered if anyone else could hear it. He hoped not. Secretly, he believed that the footsteps might be Alice and Sixteen and everyone else who had disappeared. But he knew no one else would think that. They would think it was a marauding army and they would want to run like spooked cats into the dark.

'Can anyone else hear that?' Kevin asked. 'It sounds like people are coming.'

'That's me,' Casper said. 'It's just me.'

'I can hear something too,' Diana said. 'It sounds like feet.'

Casper rapidly sprinted on the spot. 'Sorry,' he said. 'It's me.'

'No, it's not you.'

'It definitely is me.'

'It's getting louder,' Ryan said. And it was. It was getting a lot louder and closer sounding. 'It's a stampede of wildebeest.'

'No it isn't.'

'RUN.'

They ran blindly onward. The static of so many feet pounding away behind them drove them on. They ran until they reached a door standing alone in the empty space. They all piled through the door and pressed their fingers to their lips.

*

J23 gestured for everyone to stop. Everyone meant four people. The others had been swallowed by fire. For most it came as a relief. It confirmed what they already knew; everything was over and they were dead.

A black doorframe with a red door inside it stood devoid of any building, lit from above by a bare bulb. He took two steps forward and knocked. A scurrying could be heard from behind the door.

'Don't answer it,' a voice said. 'If you answer, it I'll eat you.'

'But it might be angels.'

'It's never angels. It's ghosts.'

'Angels are ghosts too.'

'We can hear you,' J23 said. 'We're not ghosts.' A baguette shot out of the letter slot and jabbed him in the belly.

'Stop eavesdropping.'

'Is Avery in there? Can you send Avery out?'

'You can have him.'

The door opened slightly and Avery was shunted out. He looked surprised. He looked up. 'Crispin?' he said. 'It worked.'

'Thank you for setting our home on fire and forcing us into the unknown.'

'I don't get it.'

'It's a thing we do sometimes. Are your friends coming out?'

'Everyone come out. They're not ghosts. They're hairy people from The Jungle.'

Casper recognized Crispin immediately. He ran to him and hugged him. 'What are you doing?' Crispin asked.

'You're my grandfather. We're a family now. We can do family things.'

'I don't want to do that.'

'Yes you do.'

'We should start moving. I don't know where this goes but I think we're supposed to follow it.'

*

They walked until the volume of their collective moaning reached a potentially dangerous level. Anything might hear them. Anything might appear in the dark.

Camp was set up beside the path. Trailers, packs, and coats were arranged into a circle and Billions arranged themselves inside of it.

Crispin and Shape cooked a full bedtime breakfast. Sausages, eggs, beans, bacon, toast, tomatoes. Crispin taught him to how to time everything so that nothing was ready before anything else.

After dinner, milk was opened and people took it in turns to make speeches over the fire.

Crispin the Great: To the one that looks like me, I don't think I'm your grandfather and I'd appreciate if you stopped trying to kiss me.

Unnamed L: If anyone lives longer than I do, please dismantle my body and feed it to parakeets.

President Captain: Listen, something very bad is probably going to happen next. We're probably not going to see each other again. We're probably going to die in different places. That's okay. I liked running away from things with you.

Billions clapped.

They rolled themselves into duvet cocoons and fell asleep.

A,

It's late. It's dark. I'm on the beach drinking beer. Singing. Skimming stones. No one else is here. The moon is. Kevin's asleep in the house. He got drunk. And cried. He said we were too far away. I didn't know what he meant.

We spent today finding out where people from school were. A lot of them are distant.

Ryan and Neil are both openly gay. They're the caretakers of an island off the coast of Scotland.

Maura teaches English in Tokyo.

Diana is an editor for a small publisher who focus on books that take place 'outside of time.'

Crispin writes articles in the form of lists for a website visited by people who are at work but don't want to be.

Pele died in a fire started by a sleepy cigarette.

Avery is a courtroom artist in Birmingham.

What else?

I'm gaining weight.

And learning to speak Dhivehi.

Pedro's baby came out of Pedro's girlfriend. It looks like an alien. He says it feels like there's an invisible blanket covering the three of them now. Their Us got bigger.

I'm in an Us with Kevin and the turtles.

Who's in yours?

I guess you aren't going to reply. I guess I didn't expect you to. It might be an old email address. You might just not want to answer.

It's okay here anyway. It's calm. We pick up turtles. We throw them back into the ocean,

C

Twelve.

Casper was the last to wake. He was the last to notice that the encampment was now surrounded by a wall of shins. The shins stretched so high that the knees they were connected to were not visible. Most of them were marked with aquamarine bruises the size and shape of trees.

Everyone was shaking. Crispin pressed a finger to his lips. He slid a piece of paper to Casper.

We're going to fight them. We're bigger than you are. We'll make distractions while you slip through the gaps.

He had been the first to wake up and the person who decided that this would be the plan. The other L had agreed. They couldn't see a future and didn't mind. They'd hidden long enough.

Casper wrote on the paper and passed it back.

No.

He wanted to stay with Crispin until he admitted he was his grandfather and did something grandfatherly.

Yes.

No.

There weren't many people left and Casper didn't want to lose more. If he was going to lose anyone, he wanted it to be himself.

Yes.

No.

I am the worst grandfather in the world and I want to help you.

Casper swallowed. He surveyed his remaining friends. They were gripping each other, eyes darting like fish between the legs around them. He nodded. The L readied their spears.

*

In the onslaught that followed, everyone lost everyone else. Billions sprinted in every direction. Spears flew. Deep voices rained from above. Blood gushed from holes. Crispin held the foot pressing down on his skull until he couldn't. His brain was crushed to a map of who he'd been between his feet. Diana coaxed a pair of knees into her face. Kelis died over Avery. Avery died under Kelis.

*

Casper regained consciousness. He yawned. They're all gone, he thought. The path was still there.

There was nothing to do but carry on.

He thought about Alice as he walked. He thought about Alice in a box and Alice in a shower and Alice eating scones on a roof in late afternoon. He clenched his fists and tried to wish her back.

He thought of futures with her in them and futures without her in them. He thought of Sixteen and leek sausages and plastic babies. His shoulders gained weight. He walked until his knuckles hung level with his ankles. He walked through a billion sky changes. I'm the only real person in this world, he thought, wondering if the others had thought the same.

A door appeared.

The door was diamond shaped and glowing green. Casper pushed through it and found himself surrounded by unending yellow. Okay, he thought. I don't mind. Grass rolled out under his feet. A giant bigger than everything took two steps forward. The owner of the feet and the hands and the voices. Casper was level with the giant's ankle. A hand reached down to pluck him from the ground and examine him. The giant's face looked like a planet to Casper.

'Let me down,' he said. 'Please.'

'Why?' The giant's voice was soft and slow.

'You killed everyone and you crushed the town and now you're going to eat me.'

'I didn't crush anything.'

'Yes you did. I saw you.'

'I'm sorry,' the giant said, sitting down. 'I didn't mean to.'

Casper hugged his knees. He looked into the giant's eye and felt suddenly very tired. 'But you killed everyone.'

'Nobody died. They all came through here. A long time ago. You're the last. I've been waiting.'

'And Alice?'

'Alice too.'

'Where did they go?'

'I don't know.' The giant shrugged. Casper was thrown into the air. He landed safely back on the giant's palm. 'Other places.'

'I'm tired.'

'I know.'

'Can I sleep in your hair?'

'Yes. But only for a while. After that, you'll have to go to other places too.'

Thanks.

Thanks Renata. Thanks Jan. Thanks Crispin. Thanks Michael.